Do you someone else's shoes?

In Her Shoes...

Modern-day Cinderellas get their grooms!

Now you can with Harlequin® Romance's
miniseries brimming with contemporary,
feel-good stories.

Our modern-day Cinderellas swap glass slippers
for stylish stilettos!

So follow each footstep through makeover to marriage,
rags to riches, as these women fulfill their
hopes and dreams....

Look out for more In Her Shoes...
stories coming soon!

Dear Reader,

Sometimes when a man seems so strong, we wonder if he's invincible. But then we get to know him and realize that somewhere, underneath the strength and determination, there are emotions and tender feelings that are perhaps even harder for him to acknowledge because it's his job to be self-contained and in control.

This is how I feel about my hero, Troy Rushton. He's lost the army career that defined so much of who he is. He's starting over, and not too keen to let others in as he does that. Yet Stacie Wakefield doesn't seem to focus on his limp, or the things that Troy *can't* do.

In fact, Troy wonders if anything would stop this intrepid, determined girl in her own life. She sews her dog clothes and carries out her DIY projects on her cottage outside of town and seems determined to forge a life by herself, and Troy… can't help admiring her. Stacie has been hurt, too. Someone very close to her found happiness at the expense of Stacie's own. It's hard for her to accept that, but Stacie hopes that starting over in a new town will help.

Though Tarrula is a fictitious town, it has a lot in common with many of the rural New South Wales towns I've lived in and visited. There is peace to be found in this small community, if Troy and Stacie can open up to each other and allow that to happen.

I hope you enjoy Troy and Stacie's journey as they find their once-upon-a-time happy ending, right in the heart of Tarrula.

Please visit my website for further information about all of my stories.

With love from Australia,

Jennie

JENNIE ADAMS
His Plain-Jane Cinderella

TORONTO NEW YORK LONDON
AMSTERDAM PARIS SYDNEY HAMBURG
STOCKHOLM ATHENS TOKYO MILAN MADRID
PRAGUE WARSAW BUDAPEST AUCKLAND

ISBN-13: 978-0-373-17792-9

HIS PLAIN-JANE CINDERELLA

First North American Publication 2012

First published in the U.K. under the title ONCE UPON A TIME IN TARRULA.

Australian author **Jennie Adams** grew up in a rambling farmhouse surrounded by books and people who loved reading them. She decided at a young age to be a writer, but it took many years and a lot of scenic detours before she sat down to pen her first romance novel. Jennie has worked in a number of careers and voluntary positions, including transcription typist and preschool assistant. She is the proud mother of three fabulous adult children, and makes her home in a small inland city in New South Wales. In her leisure time Jennie loves long, rambling walks, discovering new music, starting knitting projects that she rarely finishes, chatting with friends, trips to the movies and new dining experiences.

Jennie loves to hear from her readers, and can be contacted via her website, www.jennieadams.net.

Books by Jennie Adams

SURPRISE: OUTBACK PROPOSAL
WHAT'S A HOUSEKEEPER TO DO?
PASSIONATE CHEF, ICE QUEEN BOSS

Other titles by this author available in ebook format.

For my girls. Special mention must be made of such bald-faced justifications as: "I know you warned me about those dips in the road but I forgot again."

For Valerie, for the brainstorming that resulted in the Bow-wow-tique.

And for my editor Joanne Grant with thanks for helping me to find the greater strength in each and every book.

CHAPTER ONE

'LISTEN, Stace, I don't know how this happened. I only turned my back for a minute.'

'You were discussing football scores and you stopped watching what was happening on the floor. You can't do that when you're in charge, Gary.' Stacie Wakefield cut off the words of the assistant floor-boss of the hulling section of the almond-processing plant. 'Carl's not here. That means you're in charge!'

They stood ankle-deep in spilled harvested almonds. Stacie had spotted the problem from the office upstairs and rushed down in time for the overload to pour onto the floor. 'You may have stopped the spillage but look at it, Gary. Another five minutes and this section will be so far behind that the rest of the plant will have to wait for product. Just because Carl isn't here today, doesn't mean—'

'All right, maybe I did get distracted.' The words were mumbled before he shook his head. 'Look, I'll get it sorted out, so don't stress, okay? I'd noticed the problem by the time you got down here, hadn't I?' Gary gave her a wink and a nudge as though to convince her he was quite calm about this glitch, and that she should be too.

'You noticed too late.' Stacie muttered the words, and added more loudly, 'I hope you *can* get it sorted out.'

'It'll be all right. Well, gotta get moving.' Gary's gaze shifted behind her left shoulder. 'Time's money.'

With these words, he strode away.

Why had he done that all of a sudden after standing about, wasting time, playing down the mess to Stacie first? Because the new owner was approaching from behind her, that was why!

If that weren't the case, Stacie would eat the latest doggy coat she'd created for her home-based business, the Bow-wow-tique. Well, maybe not the dark-green one she'd made last week, but she'd added that to Fang's winter collection so it didn't really count.

New owner, Stacie.

He's not going to go away and come back at a more convenient time just because you don't want him to see this spill on the floor—or because none of this is your responsibility but Carl's asked you to take care of the new boss.

In the end it was only a meet and greet. If the owner needed anything outside of Stacie's knowledge or authority, she'd let him know what she could and couldn't do and manage.

Stacie pinned on what she hoped was a calm, helpful expression, and turned to face…

Six foot of sandy-haired, muscular man who was indeed headed her way. In fact, he was only a couple of steps from reaching her.

She fought for control against a widening of her eyes as she took in a broad chest that seemed to fill her vision: shoulders encased in a fitted white T-shirt with a corduroy tan jacket pulled over the top; blue jeans; work boots.

He had a square jaw, straight nose. His features and his attitude denoted strength, presence.

Her gaze shifted to his mouth, to a set of lips that could only have been made for long, slow kisses. His eyes were a deep hazel, green, blue and grey fringed with sooty lashes. At the moment, they were examining her with focused attention.

This was a man who would not turn his back on a challenge, nor step away if things became difficult.

Had he seen Gary's nudge and wink? Had he heard Gary's parting words?

As for the new owner, what was Stacie doing, thinking of kisses? And of 'strong' and 'tough' as something appealing and way too interesting?

It was thanks to the actions of her ex-boyfriend four months ago, thanks to a number of disappointments in that department over the years culminating in such hurt. Thanks to two people Stacie had loved that she shouldn't be thinking of any such things.

Her chin jutted. She had chosen to be single now and she would be far happier alone. That was her resolution, and already she was happier!

And what she'd noted of the new plant-owner's appeal had been an 'observation' style of thought. Only that!

'Hello.' She cleared her throat against the breathy tone that had suddenly invaded it. Dust in the air, probably. Well, maybe not. It was a clean plant.

Just get on with it, Stacie.

'You're the new owner? I'm Stacie Wakefield, the administrative assistant here.' She stuck out her hand. He probably had a wife at home enjoying those kisses, or a steady girlfriend. Of course there'd be someone. Just as, for Stacie, there'd been a sister waiting...

Thinking about that wouldn't help her.

Embrace her fresh start. That was what Stacie wanted to do.

And she was doing it!

She'd moved here to the township of Tarrula, positioned as a stopover destination between Sydney and Melbourne, and had got this job to keep her going while she built up her home business until she could live independently from it. And while Stacie was employed here at the plant, even if it was really just typing, filing and answering the phone, she would give the job her best. 'Carl apologised that he couldn't be here to officially welcome you this morning. He's unwell, but expects to be back on deck tomorrow.'

The manager had come down with a migraine at the last minute before work this morning.

'Then I'll be staying longer than I'd intended today to fill the managerial gap. Troy Rushton.' Broad, capable fingers closed around hers.

Just like that, he embraced the situation and took ownership of it.

'Stacie…' she started, and stopped because she'd already told him her name.

Nerves; this tingling in her fingers had to be nerves; the buzzing in her brain that made her lose the thread of the conversation must be from the same source. Stacie wanted to make a good impression on the new owner. She valued her job. The spill had stressed her out. She was off-centre because Carl had phoned in sick at the last moment.

As Stacie dropped her hand away, she got as far as smoothing her navy pencil-pleat skirt and stopped herself. She was perfectly presentable, if not in any way stunning.

She kind of wished she hadn't included the iridescent pink stick-ons over her blue nail-polish today, though. But her nails were her one indulgence in terms of beauty efforts. Short, but rarely forgettable.

When they had all been younger, her sisters had said her nail-decorating choices were 'tacky' and 'so not sexy, Stacie'. Two beautiful Cinderellas and one very plain duck.

The 'gorgeous' genes had gone to those older sisters. That hadn't mattered until Andrew and Gemma.

'I see there's a problem here. Who's the floor manager today?' Troy's gaze searched her face, skimmed over nose, mouth and eyes and the straight brown hair that fell to the middle of her shoulders.

Stacie thought he might have paused; was that a flicker of interest?

A moment later Troy's gaze turned to the troubled production area. He probably hadn't even noticed what she looked like, let alone had any other reaction. How silly she was being—silly on two levels, because she shouldn't be aware of him in the first place. Stacie was done with putting herself on the line with all of that.

And she hadn't truly faced up to any of the hurt of the situation she'd tried to leave behind when she'd moved here.

Stacie had been back for a visit with the family. What more was she expected to do?

Visit when Andrew and Gemma were there.

'Gary's just over here.' Stacie led the way towards the assistant floor-manager. She was very busy. There wouldn't be a lot of time to visit family in upcoming months at all.

Troy Rushton's left leg caused a limp as he walked at her side, and his expression seemed to tighten. Not in pain, but perhaps in frustration.

Was that a permanent injury? What was Troy's history? What had brought him to this small New South

Wales town and to this processing plant? Stacie had so many questions about him, but some curiosity was to be expected. He was the new owner. And gorgeous to go with it in a brooding, tough-looking way. 'I'll fill you in on plant operations as best I can, and if you need any information to help you or your family get settled here...'

'No family.' His words were a flat statement with no emotion attached that Stacie could discern. 'And the rest will wait until this production situation is sorted out.'

Right. So he was single. That was irrelevant, of course.

With an almost imperceptible nod, Stacie stopped at Gary's side. 'Gary, this is our new owner, Troy Rushton. Mr Rushton, please meet Gary Henderson.'

'Henderson.' Troy shook Gary's hand and then his eyes narrowed as he looked about them. 'What's going on?'

Gary lifted a hand to the back of his neck. 'We, ah, we had a machinery choke.'

'Why?'

It was just one word, but asked in a brooks-no-excuses tone.

'I'll get back to the office,' Stacie put in quickly.

Troy acknowledged her words with a brief glance, and Gary's with a narrowing of his eyes. He stepped further into the production area. 'Let's get this cleaned up. Then we'll finish this discussion.' To Stacie he said, 'I'll be up there shortly.'

Stacie made her way upstairs to the offices. By the time she'd put the kettle on in the little kitchenette and returned to her desk, Troy had walked in.

The office space suddenly became more vibrant, more alive.

Oh, Stacie. Why think like that?

For no good reason. That was why. And that lack of good reason needed to sort itself out right now. 'Would you like a hot drink while I take you through things up here?'

'No thanks. But in Carl's absence let's tackle the necessities. Bring whatever work you have, and a note-pad.' He crossed the open-plan area to the manager's desk and sat as though he belonged there.

He did look right there, sitting in Carl's chair. But he also looked vital and a lot younger than Carl. A man that every woman in town would fall for, Stacie decided.

Not her, though. She was immune.

Well, men seemed to be immune to sticking around with her. Andrew, anyway. And others who'd been dazzled by her sisters.

Not the point, Stacie.

No, it wasn't. And she'd made a life choice for herself now. She'd moved forward: new town, new job, new goals.

And all the old baggage to go along with it, because she couldn't just make that situation go away.

Fine; so she'd ignore it to death by focusing on this new life, and right now on the situation at hand. 'The problem down there…?'

'Is sorted out, and perhaps might not have been if you hadn't spotted it as quickly as you did.' His gaze met hers.

'How do you know?'

'I don't miss things.'

'Things don't usually fall apart on the floor if Carl isn't around.' It felt important to make that clear. 'It's just a shame they did this time.'

'Henderson was left holding—'

'The bag of almonds?' The quip escaped her.

Troy's brows rose and then his face eased into the first hint of a devastating smile. 'Yes. So to speak.'

When his face softened, there was a tiny start of a dimple in his right cheek. Stacie rather thought she might like to see that dimple fully formed.

The thought unnerved her. It would be foolish to want such a thing.

'From what I know here, the plant doesn't often have spills like that one.' And, from the sounds of it, Gary Henderson would now know he'd need to be more vigilant in the future.

'I'm glad to hear that.' When Troy looked away, it was a slow slide in time as his gaze shifted from the blue of her eyes, over her nose, before lingering on her mouth.

He blinked and a mask came down over his face.

It hadn't meant anything in particular. He was simply looking. Leave it to her gorgeous sisters to attract the genuine interest.

And leave it to Stacie to not want to attract any attention at all now. She was far better off that way!

Troy Rushton watched expressions chase themselves across Stacie Wakefield's narrow, expressive face: curiosity, interest, a certain level of consciousness of him that she felt but that she also fought.

He, too, had been drawn to her—yet what was it that drew his attention to this woman?

Was it the blue eyes with their shards of darker colour and thick, black lashes? The delicateness of her features? The soft pink of her lips? Or was it more about her expressiveness, the progression of her thoughts across her face that she probably thought she was hiding?

Whatever the reasons, he shouldn't be watching Stacie Wakefield with anything beyond a passing interest.

Indeed, he hadn't been interested in a woman since the break with Linda six months ago.

'How long have you worked at the plant, Stacie?' That was the focus of this morning, to get to know as much as possible about this processing plant he'd purchased, make sure it was functioning as solidly as it could—then move on to maintaining an ownership role while he focused most of his time and effort on his orchards.

All a far cry from army special-ops.

The thought slipped in with an edge that was too close to bitterness to be comfortable. He'd done the self-talk about this. He should consider himself lucky.

He should also consider that he didn't exactly have as much to offer a woman these days. Now why did that thought drop into his head?

'I've only been here four months.' Stacie's gaze remained steady on his face.

Had she spotted his limp?

What did it matter? It was just a part of him now.

A part that ended your career and that you despise every day.

Stacie went on. 'Carl said you visited while the plant was shut down one weekend?'

'I did, but only after I'd toured a similar plant and studied it in full action.' His visit here had been thorough enough for him to easily see that this was the better purchase.

Stacie nodded. She drew a breath and launched into the work at hand.

An expanse of utilitarian desk separated them, yet Troy still felt the imprint of her small hand from when he'd briefly clasped it. He flattened his fingers on the desk surface and pushed the thoughts aside as they moved into discussion of various matters that Stacie felt would benefit from attention today, rather than when Carl returned.

Even as they worked together, Troy wondered what had brought her to the plant. Had she moved to Tarrula, or simply changed jobs within the town? In either case, why?

It took an hour to deal with everything. At first she seemed uneasy without Carl's presence, but she soon came to terms with Troy's no-nonsense approach to decision-making and relaxed into it. As they finished, she glanced up and smiled. 'You've just made Carl's absence today very easy for me. It's the first time he's been away for a sick day since I started. I was a bit uneasy.'

'You've done just fine.'

She wasn't a gorgeous girl, Troy supposed, not by the rest of the world's standards, but her smile lit her whole face. It made him want to reach out and trace her lips with his fingertips.

The whimsical thought was so alien to his soldier's nature that Troy frowned. Even with Linda, his thoughts had tended towards the practical: shared work-interests and the meeting of physical needs. He'd cared for her, of course he had, but he wasn't what you'd call a tender man. Linda had been career-driven, and Troy had lost his career...

Troy got to his feet—one that stood as solidly and

firmly as ever, the other that didn't. 'I'll leave you now. I want to meet the rest of the crew.'

'Thanks for your help. I'll have letters for signature ready soon.' Stacie busied herself at her desk.

Troy moved towards the door. He did his best not to think about the uneven gait that got him there, but it dogged every step. 'I'll check in with you again before I leave, to sign the letters.'

He walked out.

CHAPTER TWO

'IT's good to be almost home.' Stacie spoke aloud as she slowed for a low narrow bridge. Gurudhaany Creek flowed beneath it, a muddy flow just feet deep in the summer months, but now during winter it was almost a smaller version of the large river that flowed around the outskirts of the township of Tarrula. The creek was named after the goannas that had been spotted along its banks, though Stacie had yet to see one of the large lizards for herself.

Instead today she'd met a very attractive specimen of a man, the new company owner, Troy Rushton. His imprint still seemed glued to her retinas, and that was not a fact that pleased her or that even made sense to her. 'I might need a double dose of nail-polish and some better stick-ons to get my focus off that man.'

Usually by now her thoughts would be centred on getting home, taking care of her dog, Fang, and settling in for an evening of work on her Bow-wow-tique sewing and marketing.

Instead, thoughts of Troy Rushton distracted her.

Stacie didn't want to be distracted. Deep inside where she might not have entirely faced up to a few things, Stacie emotionally couldn't afford to be distracted.

Stacie parked her grey sedan, got out and stepped through the farmhouse gate. She had faced things. She was building a new life. If that wasn't dealing with her demons, she didn't know what would be.

Visiting the family when Gemma and Andrew would be there?

It was the second time the thought had surfaced. Frankly, she didn't appreciate it.

'Did you miss me, Fang?' Stacie called out with determined good cheer. Because she was happy, damn it, and she intended to stay that way, not wallow around in thoughts of the past.

Forget thinking too much about a certain new employer, also, even if the man somehow seemed to have lodged himself firmly in Stacie's brain from the first moment she met him this morning. He wasn't *that* appealing or interesting. If Stacie had worked today with half an eye on the production floor—and specifically on Troy as he'd moved through that floor briefly greeting workers and basically rolling his sleeves up and getting involved—she'd done so to make sure the new owner didn't need her assistance with anything. Yes. It had been because of that.

'Wroof!'

Fang leaped about the yard like the happy, muscly, extremely well-dressed dog he was. He wore a pinksateen padded coat with a matching pink-studded collar. If pets could be fashion conscious, Fang really did wear his clothes with a certain pride. Stacie created them for him with pride. And with her goals for the Bow-wow-tique as firmly fixed as each stitch.

'Come on, Fang. Let's get some warmth happening inside.'

It was the start of June and the Australian winter season had hit hard. Even as Stacie headed for the farmhouse rain started to drizzle again. Stacie turned the heaters on, and then stood on the front porch and leaned down to rub the top of Fang's head and let herself absorb the blind devotion in his doggy gaze.

'Wroof!'

Fang broke away from her and ran around the little farmlet's front yard, just because he could.

Stacie laughed and then she looked up as Fang's woof changed to one of enquiry.

There was a man at the end of the path. A familiar man. Stacie's heart-rate lifted before she could even register the response. She rushed forward. 'Troy. I didn't expect— Is there something? Is production at the plant…?'

She got that far and stopped, because of course this wasn't about production at the plant. Everything had been fine when she left. Production had been closed down for the night.

Stacie's glance shifted behind Troy, to the empty farmhouse on the neighbouring property. Except it wasn't empty any more. There were lights on over there and a black four-wheel-drive jeep parked out the front.

And Troy was here on foot, as though he'd walked from somewhere quite nearby.

You do the maths, Stacie. He must have moved in next door while she'd been away at the weekend!

She'd visited her family for the first time since she'd left. She'd not enjoyed the visit and had arrived home last night and immersed herself in sewing until she forgot it. And that was without her sister's presence there, because Stacie had known Gemma was going away.

'Have you purchased Cooper's Farm? Or leased it?' She cleared her throat, cleared away those thoughts too. They were the last things Stacie wanted on her mind right now. 'I don't mean to pry. I just meant to ask, have you moved there?'

'I've bought the place.' One side of his mouth kicked up. 'With the help of the bank, that is. We did a package deal for this place and the processing plant.'

'It's a large orchard.' The trees needed work. Stacie had noted that fact when she moved in next door. 'Do you know about running an orchard? Will you be able…?'

'I can do as much work as anyone.' For just a moment, frustration seemed to bubble inside him.

'I was wondering about you finding workers.' And why he'd taken on an orchard at all.

She hadn't meant to question his physical abilities. That just really hadn't occurred to her, because he was so strong and able. Stacie thought about explaining, but it was probably best to say nothing on the topic. 'Did you grow up in a similar environment?'

'My late uncle had almond orchards.' He seemed as though he might stop here, but after a moment he went on. 'I worked there as a teenager.'

'That's good. You'll know exactly what to do, then. I didn't see you move in. When we met this morning at the plant, I didn't know...' That he would be her new neighbour.

That instead of potentially seeing him here and there when he happened to visit the plant, or if she bumped into him in town, she might see him very often. Daily...

'I moved in at the weekend. Actually, I thought your place was empty.' He cleared his throat. 'Ah, that is...'

'It seems I'm living in a place that needs a little attention?' She grinned and found her equilibrium again as she contemplated the hard work ahead. And the fulfilment of achieving her business goals, providing a home for herself, going forward by herself.

'The house needs a lot of work, but it's already habitable. It has heating and a working kitchen and bathroom, even if both are old. The foundations and structure are solid. I might strip a lot of it back to those bare bones but it will be a great place once that work is done. I've already renovated the laundry room and done a really good job of it, if I say so myself.'

She'd started there to make sure she could do the work using do-it-yourself guides and she'd proved that she could.

'In any case, welcome to your farm, and to the town, Troy.' She drew a breath. 'I should have said that this morning. I've been happy since I moved here. I hope you will be, too.'

'Thanks. I'm pleased to have the plant as an investment, though it's the orchards where I want to put in most of my time. Labour-intensive work that I do for myself.'

'Yes. The plant is a solid place, but it's not all that exciting.' As the words emerged, she clapped a hand over her mouth. 'I'm so sorry. I didn't mean...'

His eyes narrowed. For a moment she thought a rebuke might follow. It would be well deserved. What had she been thinking? Well, that she'd taken on a job that wouldn't be too taxing so she saved most of her energy for building her home business, actually—but it wouldn't be particularly PC to hint at that!

But Troy simply dipped his head. Was there a tiny hint of amusement in the back of his eyes before he did so? 'That's probably an accurate statement. Why didn't I see you over the weekend while I was moving in, Stacie?' He glanced beyond her to her home. 'I thought the place was not only empty but, eh...'

'Just an abandoned shack? The whole farmlet was a

mess when I bought it. You should have seen the yard before I put the time in to get the "jungle" hacked back to discover what garden might be left underneath. And the paddocks were terrible.'

She only had two, and they were small, but her face broke into a smile as she remembered hiring a little machine one day to get them cut down.

This move had been good for her. It had given her a new focus, and she'd needed that. She would never forget what had happened with Andrew, and because Gemma was her sister it would always be there, but Stacie didn't want to think about it all the time either.

'I haven't minded roughing it here, and the house is clean and mostly functional.' She followed his gaze to the exposed weatherboards, to the front door that needed to be realigned, to guttering that maybe needed some attention, and a few other things.

Well, a lot of things, but she had an aim for this home and at least it would keep her busy. 'I've been learning all about DIY.' And she was glad Troy hadn't minded her suggesting the plant wasn't the most exciting place to work.

'I've indulged in a few do-it-yourself projects myself. They are satisfying.'

'That's how I see it.' Stacie rushed on. 'There'll be a chicken coop one day, and a vegetable garden. I do need some work from a few tradespeople in the town. There's only one roof guy; he's been out here once.'

Stacie had been in town at that time, and disappointed

not to get up there with him to look. 'The roof needs to be treated where there are rusty patches. He fixed a few loose sheets of tin and said the rest of the work can wait until he can fit the job in. And, to answer your question, I spent last weekend away visiting family.'

'I hope you enjoyed the time with your family.' His expression made it clear that he expected she would have.

'Of course.' She said it too quickly, with too much emphasis.

Stacie sought for a change in the topic. 'Do you see your family often?'

'Not often. My parents are early retirees. They spend a lot of their time travelling.' He shifted his arm almost awkwardly. 'I couldn't say we're close.'

Stacie couldn't claim to be close to her younger sister either. Not any more. Maybe never again, but she kept the words to herself. Why was Troy not close to his parents? Was that why he'd spent school holidays with an old uncle?

'The reason I came over...' Troy shifted and she realised he had something tucked into the crook of his arm. That something wriggled and let out a yip.

'You stopped by because you have a dog?' Somehow Stacie hadn't pictured him with a pet. He seemed too *solitary* for that.

Why had he brought the dog to her? Had he learned somehow of the Bow-wow-tique and he wanted to make a purchase?

Fang would have known about the dog from the moment he let out that woof, of course.

'I found this mutt on my front step when I got home this evening. I thought it must have come from here.' Troy's words were dry, though his hold on the dog was gentle enough. 'I—' His gaze seemed to catch on her mouth before he cleared his throat and went on. 'When I saw a car arrive here I thought I'd found the dog's owner.' Troy held the bundle out. 'I'm not quite sure where it's come from if it isn't yours.'

Stacie's hands closed around it.

It was a sweet little dog, collarless and a bit too lean. It looked as though it had some poodle in its gene pool. 'It's not exactly the kind of dog I'd have pictured you owning, now that I look at him. If anything I'd see you with—I don't know—a husky or boxer or Dobermann or something.' A strong dog, a man's dog, worthy of someone like Troy.

She paused and added, 'Then again, I have Fang, and he probably doesn't exactly suit my image either, though he's a very *sweet* muscle-dog.' Even if he was terrified of balloons and grasshoppers. Stacie would keep those secrets safe for her pet!

Her gaze moved from the poodle to the much-loved Fang who was now running about her yard. She met Troy's eyes again. 'Would you like to come inside? I'm sorry I can't claim ownership of the little dog, but maybe we can clean him up and find him some food while you decide what you're going to do about him.'

His frown remained fixed. 'The owner will have to be found.'

That might not be as easy as he hoped it would be.

'How about we take care of his immediate needs for starters?' She stroked her fingers over the dog's head. It shivered in her hold. 'Food, clean it up and warmth. Once those things are sorted out, we can worry about the rest.'

Troy seemed to hesitate for a moment before he nodded. 'If you have some dog food you could spare, I'd appreciate it. Then I think I'd best take it into town to the lost-dog shelter, or the pound if there isn't one of those. That seems the logical next step.'

In a town the size of Tarrula would there be an animal shelter? And what if the pound put the dog onto borrowed time?

'We'll see what's in the phone book.' Stacie placed the dog back into his hands and led the way inside.

Troy followed Stacie into her home. The farmhouse was small, but with verandas down each side and a porch at the front. She would have her work cut out, whipping this home into shape, but it felt solid beneath his feet.

Troy had his own challenges with a dog suddenly showing up, a home and orchards to settle into and a catch-up needed with Carl Withers to discuss the forward progress of the processing plant. Yet all he could think of in this moment was the woman in front of him.

Her eyes had softened as she looked at the mutt. She'd reached for it and cuddled it close.

Stacie Wakefield was gentle, and probably a very giving woman. Troy had never looked for those characteristics, but something about those facts attracted him to Stacie in a way he couldn't explain. Strength was his forte. He'd hurt a gentle woman like Stacie, would stomp on her emotions without meaning to.

He'd never managed closeness with his parents, had much preferred the company of his crusty, grumpy, unemotional old uncle until the man had died while Troy was away on a mission. Even then he hadn't missed him, not desperately. Just those times of quiet companionship with Les had counted the most.

'Come inside, Troy.' Stacie gestured him into her home.

Visions of Stacie working about the place filled Troy's mind, filled it with too much curiosity and interest. He could picture her in old clothes or overalls, intrepidly taking on DIY projects, strange nail-decorations flashing as she worked. He stifled a smile.

And he had to admit the combination of delicacy and determination that he sensed in Stacie intrigued him whether he wanted to let it or not.

'Bring the dog into the laundry. We might as well start with a bath for it.' Stacie led the way.

As Troy followed, her dog trotted into the house behind them. Rather than greet Troy with a territorial, warning growl, it wriggled against Stacie's legs and gave a happy woof, and then became even more excited when it looked at the fellow canine in Troy's hold.

The poodle froze for a moment and sniffed the air, but apparently decided it was safe with Fang, because it relaxed again in Troy's hold.

As for Fang, the beast was dressed in a pink dog-coat and matching collar. The male actually looked proud of the fact.

Troy glanced about Stacie's home. A chew toy lay in the hallway. Bright rugs covered board floors. It smelled of womanly things and home cooking, fresh paint and furniture polish. And welcome.

Those things might feel just right to some people, but to Troy they were warning signs to stay clear.

So why wasn't he feeling the urge to back away? Perhaps it was because he was here for very practical reasons. A lost dog that he needed to deal with was a nuisance, a problem that needed to be fixed. Put like that, it sounded very much like business.

Keep saying so, Rushton. Maybe you'll even believe it.

'No bath for you, Fang. Not while I take care of this little one.' Stacie bent to pet her animal.

She turned back to take the bundle of scruff out of Troy's hands. Her words, her kindness to the stray, pulled Troy back to reality. A home smelling of welcome, a soft-hearted woman, were the last things he should have on his mind. And that brought him to the mutt, and to Stacie's reaction to it.

'The dog should be checked for a microchip.' He passed the animal to her. 'It's probably got an owner out there.'

His instincts told him that wasn't true, but he wasn't going to take on a pet. To do that denoted 'making a home'. Troy was not about that.

He was happy to have a roof over his head, an investment business and the challenge of his orchards. He had no plans to emotionally attach himself to any of it.

'I understand, Troy. The dog just turned up on your doorstep. I think the water's a decent temperature now.' Stacie spoke the words as her dog sat with a woeful howl at her feet. She glanced down, and back to Troy. 'Fang loves the water. He's going to be jealous about this bath.'

Stacie stood the pseudo-poodle in the laundry tub and washed it efficiently, but not efficiently enough to avoid being liberally splashed as the dog tried to decide whether it liked this treatment or wanted to escape. Mostly the latter instinct won out.

How could a laundry, even a nicely renovated one, seem cosy and intimate with a dog in a tub and another looking reproachful on the floor, for crying out loud?

'There. I think he's all clean now.' Stacie drained the water out of the tub, holding the dog in place as she did so.

'Okay. I've got him.' Troy wrapped a towel around the dog and together they held him still while Troy rubbed the towel over him. Get the job done, and then exit out of here; that was what Troy needed to do now.

But for a moment Troy's face was bent over Stacie's nape as he reached from behind her shoulder to rub the towel over the dog's back. The temptation to drop a kiss on Stacie's soft skin swept over him.

He drew a breath and covered the thought at the same time that he lifted the small dog clear of the sink area.

Troy glanced down at the splattered front of Stacie's soft blue sweater. 'I'm not sure who ended up wearing the most of that bath, you or the dog.' If he tossed the words off, maybe they would defuse that desire to kiss her. Since when had he pined for softness? The one relationship that Troy had committed to had been with a woman employed in the armed services, and though there'd been commitment it had been a practical one. This reaction to Stacie must be some kind of glitch or something.

'I'll go and change.' Stacie glanced down too. When she looked back up, there were roses in her cheeks.

Troy's hands stilled where he held the dog. He blinked. Perhaps he lost a round of the battle, because Stacie had blushed over her water-spattered sweater. That was about the most appealing thing he'd seen in a long time, and he liked it. For all that he'd lived by his self-control, right now he couldn't seem to control that response to her.

Delicate; that was what Troy thought when he tried to come up with a word to describe her.

And in terms of outward appearance that was true. She was fine-boned, built on small lines. But Stacie was also a DIY expert in the making, someone who obviously had some physical strength and determination to go with it.

She was also beautifully shy about herself as a woman. Which of those things was responsible for this interest he felt towards her, that would surely disassemble itself any moment now?

'Yeah—eh.' He cleared his throat and stepped back, taking the wriggling bundle of dog with him. 'I'll just take the dog into your front hall; get it out of this small room and finish drying it off. It's still a bit damp.' He backed out of the room and refused to watch as Stacie made her way to her room to change her sweater.

Troy dried the animal with determined attention, Stacie's dog standing by. The smaller dog didn't appear afraid of Stacie's pet, and her dog seemed friendly enough not to mind the invasion of its turf.

'Not much of a guard dog, are you?' Troy murmured the question to the Staffie, which wagged its tail and— Troy would swear—preened in its pink outfit. It might have jaws like a vice, but a mushy heart appeared to go with them.

'That mushy heart wouldn't last ten seconds in the army.' Troy let the small dog loose.

'Oh, good, you've finished,' Stacie said as she

rejoined him. 'I checked the phone book. Tarrula doesn't appear to have an animal-rescue centre. The pound has an emergency number for after hours, but I don't think we really classify as an emergency.'

She'd changed the blue sweater for a cream one, and her work skirt for form-fitting jeans that showed every lovely curve to perfection. Just like that, all Troy's belief that he could set aside awareness of her evaporated.

Well, he must push these reactions aside. Far and fast, because Stacie was a neighbour and an employee of sorts. And Troy was sworn off women in any case.

'I guess it'll have to wait for tomorrow to be checked for a microchip. At least the dog didn't scrub up too badly.' He forced his thoughts to that. 'For a mutt.'

'High praise, indeed.' Stacie laughed.

And Troy responded to that laugh with a relaxing feeling inside himself that was wrong. All wrong!

The animal trotted into the depths of the house.

'He's headed for the kitchen.' Stacie started to follow. 'Let's find some food for both dogs.'

A radiant electric heater warmed the kitchen. Around the room, pieces of rag had been stuffed into cracks in walls that had paint peeling from them.

Stacie had put her mark on the room regardless. There were knickknacks on shelves, and the room still managed an overall welcoming feel despite the work needed.

Stacie opened an elderly cupboard in the corner and

pulled out a can of dog food. 'This should keep him going. What happens if he has no owner, Troy?'

'It'll have to go to the pound.' He looked down at the dog, which looked up at him with trusting eyes. 'Someone will want it. It's a cute thing in its way.'

And then he looked at Stacie, who also returned his gaze with an edge of militancy that thinly covered worry. 'If no one wants him, the pound will want to destroy him.'

Troy had taken lives in the line of duty. Saved children. Hunted down people who didn't care who in the world they destroyed. He'd stood by his team, his commitment and his beliefs, and had done what had to be done.

Now he faced a woman who was concerned about the future of a dog. He hadn't really thought what might happen once he handed it over. Once he regained the ability to think, he made himself reassure her. 'I'll get their commitment about that before I hand it over.'

'Thank you.' Her shoulders relaxed a little. 'For now, he needs a coat. I have one that will fit.'

'Really? Your dog isn't exactly the same size.' As Troy spoke, he didn't so much as glance in Fang's direction, but he could hardly have failed to notice the way Stacie's dog was dressed.

Stacie felt proud—of Fang's clothing, yes, but moreover of standing up for the small dog's future. That was a potential problem.

And there was another problem she was facing, that

of being far too aware of this man. Was it because he was so clearly very strong that she found it so hard to ignore his magnetism? Past boyfriends had been... softer men. Andrew, too, because even when he had chosen Gemma over Stacie he'd been self-interested rather than ruthless.

Her glance lifted to Troy's and locked there, caught in hazel depths that seemed to read every thought in her head. She sincerely hoped that wasn't so.

Then Stacie glimpsed the edge of sensual need deep in the backs of Troy's eyes.

'Well, I'd best get the coat.' She tried very hard to walk normally up the short hallway to the spare bedroom she'd converted for creating garments for the Bow-wow-tique. Yet she felt ridiculously aware of leading Troy deeper into the house, and right next door to her bedroom.

For goodness' sake, Stacie. Do you think he's going to die of shock if he sees a glimpse of bedcover or something? Or that he'll succumb to an overwhelming urge to toss you down on the bed and deliciously ravish you?

She should be more concerned about his impressions of her home business. Maybe she shouldn't have drawn his attention to it in this way, but it was too late now. She would simply have to deal with it.

Stacie pushed the door of the spare room open and stepped inside. 'This is the Bow-wow-tique. Most of what I make currently, I sell online. That will change now that I've moved here. Tarrula hosts several national dog-shows each year, and has a strong tourist industry, much of which drives straight past the entry road to the farmlet.'

To Troy's orchards, too, but they were a little further along. 'I'll be holding an open day out here a month from now and hoping to attract some of those buyers.'

She drew a breath and completed the verbal picture for him. 'I hope to be independently living off this business a year from now.'

'Leaving the job at the plant at that time.' He dipped his head. 'I can see that you're on an adventure. You've set yourself a challenge, a goal to reach for and achieve. It's very enterprising of you.'

His assessment was a little surprising, but so true. He was also very accepting of her plans. 'Yes. And… this is the hub of Bow-wow-tique.'

She glanced about the room and tried to see it through his eyes.

Her sewing machines were kept in an antique-style pullout desk-cabinet. A matching large cupboard housed fabrics and sewing notions, fastenings, rolls of ribbon, boxes of plain collars and other practical items Stacie worked with to produce her designs.

The bright colours of all sorts of coats, small blankets, basket liners and so much more were spread about the room on tables and in open cartons and gave the room a jazzy feel. Her computer sat on a small desk in the corner.

Troy stepped farther inside and let his glance rove around. 'This explains your dog's attire a little better. If you hadn't told me you make these things, I'd have thought you got them from a shop. They look perfect. You must put a lot of work in here, Stacie.'

'I do.' She got to explore her creative side.

'I think you have a good chance of succeeding.' He sounded impressed rather than concerned, so that had to be good, didn't it?

'Thank you. I hope so. Let's find a coat for this dog.' Stacie tried for a brisk tone to cover up the wash of pleasure his praise and encouragement had given her. 'Do you have heating at your new home?' The coat she picked up was chocolate brown. 'This should do.'

'I do have operational heating, yes.'

'That's good. It won't have to be cold.' Great. That sounded as though she cared about the dog, but not about Troy.

Stacie tugged the last stick-on from one blue nail. The rest had come off in the water as she bathed the dog. Maybe it was the lack of her signature nail-art that was making her words so interpretable.

And maybe she was distracted by the presence of a certain gorgeous man! 'Of course I don't want you to be cold either, Troy.'

She drew a breath. 'Well, I wouldn't mind having the dog until things get sorted out. It could be in the yard with Fang until you find out if there's an owner. Fang is good with other animals.'

'That'd be great, thanks. If you'd do that, it'd save taking it to the pound while I advertise for any owners.' Troy didn't try to talk her out of the idea. His hand rose to the back of his head. 'I don't see myself as much of a dog minder, but I'll cover all the costs for its food and lodgings.'

She thought he mumbled that he was better at manning a machine gun.

Before she could think about that, he added, 'I don't want to burden you, though.'

'It's okay.' It was more than okay, and in the end, even if he obviously didn't want the dog himself, and might not be all that attached to dogs on the whole, he was being generous. 'I don't mind having him while we figure out if there's an owner out there.'

If the answer to that question turned out to be no, they would deal with the next step at that time.

As they retraced their steps down the hallway, Troy spoke again. 'I should get back to my place. There are a few things left that didn't get done at the weekend.'

His words made Stacie realise how easily she could have lingered, talking to him, letting time drift when that was the last thing she should be doing with her new neighbour.

'And I should get on with my Bow-wow-tique work. It keeps me busy.' In the evenings, when other people would be doing things with their partners.

The thought wasn't exactly uplifting so she pushed it

away. She would also do her nails again tonight. Pink, Stacie decided, with star-and-moon stickers.

They made their way to the front of the house. Once in the foyer, she dropped to her knees. The poodle obligingly came over to sniff at her hands. She quickly got dog and coat put together and fastened up.

'Thanks for offering to keep it.' Troy stepped towards Stacie's door. 'I'll swing by early tomorrow and collect it to take it to the vet to be checked for that microchip.'

'The dog will be in the yard with Fang. If you can't raise me, or I've already left for work or anything, just take him.'

You see? That was all fine. They'd had a normal, neighbourly transaction. Now Troy was leaving and tomorrow they might see each other here or at the plant and that would be completely fine as well.

Stacie told herself all was well, and indeed she was fine until their glances met and she thought she found parts of herself in the depths of his eyes, in the way he seemed to guard himself.

Do not decide you know him, or that you share traits with him, Stacie.

All that kind of thinking could do for her was cause problems, and she didn't know the man at all. But she did know he was single.

Yes. Great one to dwell on right now, Stacie.

'I guess I might see you tomorrow morning.'

'Yeah.' He backed a step and then another. 'Have a good night.'

Troy walked back to his farm.

Stacie went through the house and Fang flopped down in front of the kitchen heater in his pink outfit, while Stacie started organising her dinner. The little poodle stayed just inside her front door. Was it watching for Troy to return? But of course Troy didn't, and eventually the dog came into the kitchen too.

Stacie sighed. 'Well, I hope Troy didn't think I was frivolous because of my creations, but he was quite supportive of my business. That's generous, really, considering I'm planning to leave my job at the plant eventually.'

True, but Troy himself was happy to own the plant and didn't want to spend all his time working there.

Stacie got on with her evening, enjoying Fang and the little dog's company, working on her Bow-wow-tique sewing and online marketing.

She didn't think about Troy at his nearby farm. She barely noticed when she happened to glance out of a window to see him go to one of the outbuildings and start shifting home-gym equipment about in there as though he really meant business with it.

Stacie draped a tape measure around her neck, repainted her nails and added the new stick-ons. She worked at her sewing some more. She didn't imagine Troy thinking of her hard at work on her hobby. As if he would spare it or her a thought. Stacie might like her fantasy nails, but in life she understood she needed to be firmly grounded in reality.

CHAPTER THREE

'I CAN'T believe I've lost Troy's dog. Well, his stray dog, but it's the same thing!' Stacie hurried the short distance from her front yard to Troy's yard. She'd been everywhere—down to the creek, through her two paddocks, along the lane that led to the road. Fang had gone with her, but he hadn't proved much worth as a sniffer dog. He'd been too busy sniffing leaves and sticks. Right now he was shut back in the yard.

Stacie pushed open the door to Troy's shed. She'd planned to casually and calmly ask for his help to search for the dog. That plan unravelled the moment she caught sight of him.

He was seated on a bench, lifting a set of weights. He had on a grey sleeveless knit-shirt, a darker-grey pair of shorts and trainers on his feet. As he moved, muscles across his upper body and in his legs and thighs flexed.

The slight breathlessness from her hurried search for the poodle suddenly became acute.

Troy was…beautiful. Absolutely toned everywhere,

with strong, defined muscles and a hardness that seemed not only to be on the outside of him, but within.

There were marks on him—a scar across one shoulder and upper arm. And on his leg lines of scar tissue above and below the knee, and the knee itself was misshapen as though pieces had shattered away.

Oh, Troy. How did this happen to you?

On the walls in the shed were photographs: men in uniform, out of uniform, carrying guns, out in the field. Troy featured in many of them. His physique had already suggested such a background. Stacie had known he'd be muscled but seeing it in this way wasn't quite the same as thinking about it. Seeing his injury… And the expression on Troy's face…

All emotion had been cleared, wiped away and replaced by utter focus presented in a sharp, closed determination. He looked controlled and ready for anything.

She'd just seen a glimpse into his world, into why ownership of a processing plant and orchards hadn't seemed to fully fit him, though she had no doubt he'd succeed at both.

Before she had time to be stunned by that glimpse into her new neighbour, even perhaps to wonder if she should feel intimidated, the concentration on Troy's face changed as he noted her entrance. He set the weights down and rose.

'I didn't mean to interrupt your routine.' She didn't

mean to stand here goggling over how magnificent he was, or to see his injury and want to hold him.

He would never allow that kind of empathy.

She'd known that even before she saw the photos on the wall that told her in stark images who he was and where he'd come from.

And what he'd lost, because he would never have chosen to step away from that army life. That truth was also tacked to his wall in those timeless images: camaraderie. Group shots with other soldiers. Training events. And real events that Stacie wasn't sure she wanted to think too much about. That was his identity and belonging. There wouldn't be room for the softer emotions in such a life.

She struggled to pull her thoughts back together. 'I came to tell you I've lost your—'

'The dog got away on you. Actually, I planned to come over once I finished my workout.' His gaze shifted to a corner of the room where a sports bag sat on the floor.

A little dog sat beside it.

'Oh, I'm so relieved that he's okay, but how did he get out of my yard? It's properly dog-proofed. I made sure of that when I first moved here, for Fang's sake.'

Troy's gaze examined the small animal. 'I don't know why he'd want to come here anyway.'

The dog had no microchip. Troy had discovered that yesterday when he'd taken it to the vet. Stacie had asked Troy to advertise locally and wait a couple of weeks before he did anything more. But the idea was for the dog to stay with her in the interim.

'Dratted poodle,' she said.

'Damned Houdini dog,' Troy said at the same time.

'Oh. That's a perfect name for him.' A smile melted Stacie's anxiety away. 'And I'll take him back, get him out of the way while you finish—'

'I'm about done, anyway.' Troy's glance moved between her and the dog. 'It's just a good way to ease the kinks out after a big day in the orchards.'

After just two days, his efforts out there were already noticeable.

In fact, she'd done rather too much noticing as Troy had gone about his work.

Now Stacie was filled with curiosity and words popped out before she could stop herself.

'Would you like to join me for dinner?' She should stay away from him, but she wanted to get to know him.

Stacie wanted to know about those army photos. That could just be a very understandable neighbourly curiosity.

Except it went much deeper than that. This man had wounds, physical wounds that had changed his life.

Just as Stacie had emotional wounds that she had to get over.

Well, she was trying.

And Troy would probably say no to coming to dinner, anyway.

Troy glanced at the dog. 'I feel I'm asking more than I should of you already.'

'I offered to mind him.' As though the rest really didn't matter, she shrugged her shoulders. 'It's just a slow-cooker meal that I put on this morning.'

He hesitated for a moment before he inclined his head. 'A home-cooked meal would be nice.'

Troy had watched Stacie's face as she invited him to dinner. He'd known he should say no to the invitation. She owed him nothing and it was better to keep to their boundaries.

But would it be so bad to spend an hour looking at…sparkling bluebells? What harm would that do, really? Provided he treated the dinner in the way it was intended.

But just how is it intended, Rushton? Is it an uncomplicated invitation? For you? And for her?

She'd seen his shattered knee. There'd been no revulsion, and no pity that he could discern. And he didn't want her pity, hers, or anyone's. She'd just offered dinner. Maybe out of guilt for losing the dog, though he would never have blamed her for that. So he would have dinner with her.

Get to know Stacie better?

Maybe. But that was a neighbourly, appropriate thing to do.

It wasn't like him to get bogged down in second-guessing things. Troy set the thoughts aside; he would go. That was all. It would be fine. 'Ten minutes?'

'Ten minutes.' A soft smile lit her face. She lifted one hand to tuck strands of silky-brown hair behind a shell-like ear.

Pink; her nail-polish was pink now.

He honed his gaze, took a step closer.

Moons and stars; Stacie had decorated her nails with far away moons and stars. She crouched to call the poodle to her and then she was gone.

Moons and stars.

Troy shook his head, and a small, appreciative smile crept across his lips.

'Thank you for this.' Troy ate another bite of the beef-and-vegetable casserole before he went on. 'It's delicious. Just the right kind of food for this cold weather. Where did you learn to cook?'

They were seated at the dining table in Stacie's kitchen. Somehow the table had never seemed quite this cosy to Stacie. Indeed, it seated four—six at a stretch. Troy's presence seemed to fill her home. Stacie felt on edge on the one hand, and oddly relaxed and happy on the other.

It must be because Troy was easy to talk to, interesting, and a sound conversationalist on a range of topics from local sports to international politics. She hadn't expected that—for him to put her at her ease with his conversation. Yet there were moments when she thought his gaze lingered on her eyes, and her breath would catch. That was such a dangerous way to feel.

Don't go there, Stacie. Don't start letting thoughts rise that have no place between you and him, and no place in your life any more at all.

She could not allow herself to be hurt again. She'd made her decision. That meant she steered clear from any possibility of those kinds of entanglements.

'Mum taught me and my sisters the basics of how to cook, and then encouraged us to explore.' Stacie took another bite of meat and slowly chewed it. 'We used to take turns picking out a dinner and making it each week when we were all teenagers. One of my favourites was a pie made of polenta and topped with grilled tomato, onion and garlic. For a man who likes meat and three veg in a fairly plain presentation, I'm not sure how Dad survived my experimental phase.'

She didn't mention that her sisters were both stunning women. Well, it wasn't relevant to this conversation, was it? And Stacie didn't resent their beauty. Of course she didn't.

She missed those family times, but what could she do?

Troy glanced at his almost empty plate. 'I can't imagine you producing anything that wasn't appealing. How many sisters do you have?'

It was just conversation, just an exchange of interest. But Stacie's tone didn't portray the simplicity it should have as she replied. 'I have two sisters. The eldest is married and the other is…involved with someone.'

Troy's gaze sharpened. He was going to ask something and Stacie didn't want him to. She didn't want to feel exposed.

In the living room beyond them, Fang rolled over in front of the electric heater and gave a doggy sigh. He seemed content with Houdini napping beside him, leaving Troy and Stacie to their heater in the kitchen.

'Would you like coffee, Troy?' Stacie got quickly to her feet and busied herself filling the jug with water.

Once they were made, they took the drinks to the living room.

Troy shook his head over the dogs and sat in one of Stacie's lounge chairs. He'd let the earlier conversation go easily, and Stacie was grateful for it.

Now he said, 'It must be nice to be that easy to please.'

'Yes. I don't think the negative tones of "it's a dog's life" apply around here.' She'd noticed the careful way that he lowered himself into the chair, so asked, 'Is your leg paining you, Troy?' Had his exercise routine earlier done that to him? Or the hard work in his orchards? She hated to think of him being uncomfortable. 'Is there anything I can do to help?'

'It's fine.' After a small silence, he sighed and admitted, 'It plays up a bit in this kind of weather. The warmth from the heater will help.'

'The cause of the injury, is it something you can talk about?' Stacie rose and adjusted the temperature on the heater up a bit. When she caught his frown, she bit her lip. 'I'm sorry, Troy. You don't have to discuss it if you don't want to. It's just that I saw all your army photos, and I thought it might have happened there. Why else would you—?'

'Leave a career I was made for?' He asked the question emotionlessly.

Yet Stacie sensed there was passion hidden behind those flat words. She'd wanted to ask, to learn more about him. Now she wondered if she'd intruded too far by doing that. She bit her lip. 'Yes. I guess that's what I wondered.'

The dogs watched her with half-asleep gazes. They were probably thinking she was foolish for bringing up a touchy subject. She returned to her chair and sank into it.

'I took a hit on a mission.' Troy's words were calm, at least on the surface. 'It happened overseas.'

Should she thank him for the information and leave it at that, or invite further discussion? Stacie wanted to *know* him, more than just the superficial things. Not in a painful way for Troy, but in a *supportive* way.

'You were in some kind of special-ops, or particularly high-risk task force, weren't you?'

That was what hadn't seemed quite ordinary about those pictures.

It was another piece of him, one that made perfect sense the moment it occurred to her.

'Yeah. But what made you think that?'

'A lucky guess?' Stacie couldn't explain to him the real reason because she wasn't sure herself. It must be his excellence, his attitude and his strength. The fact that he didn't have movie-star looks but he compelled attention, he stood out, he didn't seem like any man she had met before. That strong core that she had seen in his workout room would carry him through harsh missions and allow him to do his job.

It was also an ability to shut off his emotions. Shut them down for the better good of his work. Was that something that would only apply in terms of dangerous work he might have to do? Or did Troy apply that to other areas of his life?

Had Stacie done the same—shut herself down in some areas so she didn't have to feel?

'I've never closely known someone who had that kind of career.' That was the topic of conversation right now and Stacie would focus on that and only that. There was nothing wrong with getting to know him. The rest of it, she would worry about later when she could unravel her thoughts into something sensible!

Troy was someone trained to assess situations in less than the blink of an eye, to take hard action where necessary, to measure life in terms of artillery power when that need arose. And he did seem a very strong man, internally as well as physically.

'I imagine you'd have pushed your way to the top and that you preferred to keep your counsel about that work.'

'You're right. My job in the armed services wasn't an ordinary one.'

Then he'd been injured and had moved here to start over. 'I hope you'll be happy here, Troy.'

She didn't know how it would feel to have a work ambition, a career path, that she lost due to this kind of reason. 'I've been lucky. I've always had clerical jobs, some more demanding than others. When I decided to go after my dream of establishing the Bow-wow-tique, I chose Tarrula as my base because it's on a tourist route. It also holds the national dog-shows here each year and I was able to just take another similar job to see me through.'

'I don't think there's been anything lucky about that. I think you've set goals and are working hard to make them happen.'

'What about you, Troy?' An orchard was a far cry from an army career. 'Can you be happy?'

'I've made my choices.' His gaze held hers. 'The orchards aren't some kind of attempt at a replacement, but for my previous career I wanted the physical work and satisfaction of it. So far I'm getting that.'

'I admire you.'

He leaned forward in his chair. In a strange way, she felt as though they had more in common than she had realised, even if for very different reasons. Stacie's wounds were on the inside.

Troy had endured a physical loss that had taken away his chosen career. But there must have been emotional fallout from that, too. How strong and determined he must be to reinvent himself the way he was doing.

'I should head home, Stacie.' Troy's words were low. He got to his feet. 'Thanks for dinner and the coffee. I really enjoyed your company.'

She could have thought that she'd made him want to leave, made him uncomfortable with her questions. But a glimpse into his eyes before he shielded his gaze told differently, because there was reciprocal consciousness there.

And now he was leaving.

Troy seemed equally determined not to notice her other than in a very neighbourly way but perhaps he was finding that resistance a little difficult.

Stacie walked Troy to her front door. The little dog followed, and shot through the door the moment Stacie opened it.

Stacie called him back, and he returned, but reluctantly. He'd been headed straight for Troy's house again.

'If he knows what's good for him, he'll stay here.' Troy turned and for just a moment his gaze searched hers. 'He should realise how lucky he is to get that open-handed welcome.'

Nothing else was said, not a single word to indicate that anything had changed—but, oh, those words seemed to be about more than a Houdini poodle with a penchant for escaping. *Troy* had felt welcome. And she was glad about that.

Stacie looked into Troy's eyes, he looked into hers, and she knew that he wanted to kiss her, and that she wanted it too. They might have both done their best to ignore it, but that desire had been there since they'd met.

While her mind refused to think its way beyond that knowledge, time seemed to inexplicably slow down as Stacie yielded to his searching gaze. Troy hesitated on the threshold. His head dipped towards hers, just a little. Just enough for her to catch her breath.

She wondered how it would feel to have his lips meet hers. To be held by his strength. To hold him.

What was she thinking? Stacie *couldn't* think this way. She'd been hurt. She was still hurting. In no way could she put herself at that kind of risk emotionally again!

'I… Goodnight, Stacie. I really should go.' He straightened and took a step back. A moment later he was gone, limping into the darkness, and Stacie was inside the house. She'd walked to her sewing room before her thoughts reformed. Once they did, she stood in the centre of the room and bit her lip.

Had he truly thought about kissing her just then? He had; she hadn't imagined it.

What had happened to her great plan not to be affected in that way by him?

'You sabotaged it by inviting him to dinner, Stacie Wakefield, that's what!' She spoke out loud to force herself to acknowledge it.

CHAPTER FOUR

THREE days passed. Troy worked hard on his orchards and the time slid by, but that didn't mean he wasn't conscious of his neighbour. He'd come close to kissing her at her house the night they'd shared dinner there. Troy should never even have entertained that impulse, but he had.

Stacie had figured out things about his past vocation that night, too. She'd realised that he'd been ruthless enough to push his way to the top in a field where there was little room for emotion, and to do well in that field until injury had taken him out.

God, he missed that life. It was the only thing that had made him feel right about himself, a vocation where the emotional lack his mother had constantly bemoaned was a benefit.

'I'm sorry Carl's not here again, Troy.' Stacie's words were apologetic, professional, but also just a little breathless. Soft flags of colour stained her cheeks. 'He's out at a meeting with one of our key orchardists.'

'It's okay. I wanted to check on the plant briefly,

that's all.' Troy hadn't stopped by hoping to see her. He told himself this, but his gaze still lingered on that soft colour.

Stacie was a nice woman, kind, determined, and with her own life plan. And, if creating dog-coats and accessories as a successful home-based business seemed a rather unusual goal, it was still a very hard-working one. Particularly while she was holding down another full-time job at the same time. Troy should value her for those things and leave the rest alone.

This had never been a problem for him before. And Stacie was completely unlike any woman he'd have said might be even a halfway suitable match for him.

Linda had been the only one he'd felt was right, and she'd walked away quickly enough once it had become clear that the damage to his knee was permanent. Not that Troy would have expected anything else of her. If she hadn't made that choice, he'd have made it for her.

Yeah? So why did it sting, then?

A sting against his pride and plans, he supposed.

'Did you come to town to join in the after-work hour we've got on at the pub?' Stacie held a bunch of invoices in her hands. She shuffled them as she waited for his answer.

It was raining outside again, another light fall just audible on the roof of the building. The machinery had come to a stop on the processing floor below.

Stacie followed his glance through the plate-glass

windows to the floor. 'Most of the crew goes. It's a good social event.'

For some reason, Troy pictured Stacie with water droplets gilding her fall of straight hair. He would lift his hand and brush the droplets away...

'When I think of off-duty team-bonding exercises the ideas usually involve extreme sports and other calculated-risk activities.' But he couldn't do those now, and Stacie was waiting for his answer. 'Carl did mention this at the start of the week.'

Troy had had no intention of entering any kind of social whirl in Tarrula, work-related or otherwise, so he'd pretty much put the idea out of his mind.

Nevertheless, it might be a good opportunity to get to know staff in an informal setting. He'd briefly greeted them all on the first day, but that was about it.

'Do you go to these staff get-togethers, Stacie?' It shouldn't have been a particularly important question, yet the thought of her out at a pub with a bunch of men from the plant brought about a jealous and protective instinct in Troy that he didn't want to acknowledge. It was quite ridiculous, and one-hundred percent inappropriate.

'I go along most weeks.' Stacie shifted to start tidying the contents of her desk. 'It's usually a fun time.'

'Then we'd best get going.' The rest of the plant was quiet now. Troy started downstairs to check the building while Stacie gathered her things and secured the office for the night.

Stacie watched Troy's broad back disappear down the staircase that led from the offices, and she noticed that the descent was awkward for him. She made her way downstairs to join him and they drove separately, with Troy following Stacie as she led the way. Minutes later they walked into the pub together. It was silly, but for a moment Stacie almost felt as though they were on a date.

Sure, Stacie. A date that includes every other employee at the plant.

She mustn't think of it in that light, anyway! Yet, as she walked at Troy's side, she was very aware of him, of the breadth of strong shoulders as he moved at her side, of that uneven gait that he seemed to hate so much.

She'd seen the definition of muscles honed by years of attention to physical fitness. She'd held her breath and hoped he would kiss her, and pushed all those thoughts and reactions aside since. They threatened her equilibrium, the fragile truce she'd built with herself.

So this work hour was fine. She'd introduce Troy around again, if he wanted that. Enjoy the social outing for what it was. And she would *not* think about the appealing and intriguing aspects of him—case closed!

Stacie's sigh was audible enough that it reached Troy's ears, even in the pub's noise-filled environment. He glanced her way, and then wondered if perhaps he shouldn't have. She looked rather lovely in profile, as she had with her head bent over her desk. And when he'd nearly given in to the temptation to kiss her...

How had he missed the depth of her subtle loveliness at first? Yet even then he'd been aware of her.

Well, he would just have to stop being aware, before thoughts like that got both of them into trouble.

Troy looked around. The pub was a decent-sized place, with bistro dining in a room tucked away to the left and a separate room dedicated to poker machines. The bar was long with dark wood polished to a dull sheen and green hard-wearing carpet on the floor where it wasn't bare, wooden planks.

The smell of beer and a low buzz of after-work humanity filled the place. For a moment Troy saw another bar, another bunch of people: army mates relaxing at their favourite haunt in a Melbourne suburb they frequented when they were off-duty.

His guys. Their pub. A whole other world that had been *all* of Troy's world.

'Stace, how about a game of pool?'

'Getting a bit dry over here, Stace. How about a round of beers for us?'

A couple more calls accompanied Stacie's entry into the pub.

Stacie gave a general smile. 'Maybe a bit later. I'm busy just at present.'

As he and Stacie stepped further into the room, Troy heard one man say to another, 'She's a nice girl, but she always keeps her distance, doesn't she?'

'I reckon some bloke's hurt her along the way.'

'Nah. She seems happy enough.'

Stacie wouldn't have heard the interchange, but Troy tended to agree with the first man. He, too, suspected Stacie had withdrawn from the game because she might have been hurt in it.

She was made to be in a relationship, to share all those soft and tender emotions with someone who would welcome and appreciate them. If she'd tried that and it hadn't worked out...

Oh yes, and you'd be more suitable for that?

Of course not. Absolutely not. It would just be a shame for Stacie to go through life alone, in Troy's opinion. Although, Troy himself couldn't pursue such a path; he wouldn't have enough to offer her on that emotional level.

'Good to see you here.' Gary Henderson stepped forward, clapped Troy on the back and nudged Stacie with his elbow. 'Well done on bringing Troy along, Stace.'

'It's a nice way to end up the week, Gary.' Stacie's words were cheerful. Her glance dropped to the beer in Gary's hand. 'You're set, so I'll just get drinks for us. Troy—what would you like?'

She walked to the bar to order for both of them.

Troy spoke with Gary for a bit and then chose a table towards the back of the bar. Stacie joined him with their drinks. One and two at a time, men made their way over to speak to them. Stacie greeted each person and exchanged a few words, making Troy's second-time around getting-to-know-you job easy for him.

It was teamwork, and Troy appreciated it. But in this social setting it felt too much like dating her. That wasn't a good feeling to allow himself to drift into, yet at every moment he was utterly conscious of her.

'Stacie, how about introducing us?' The words came from a woman who approached their table.

The brunette had a load of inquisitiveness in her gaze that sharpened even more as she got a good look at Troy. 'Oh, you know what? We can do it for ourselves.'

Her glance became coy. 'I'm Aida Gregory, the sister of Dan Gregory from your plant. And you're obviously the gorgeous new plant-owner.'

The woman pulled up a chair. She laid her fingers over his arm as she offered some confidence or other.

Troy leaned back in his chair, removing himself from her reach without making the action too obvious.

'I should go mingle.' Stacie started to get to her feet.

'We both should.'

Troy would have joined her, but before either of them could move, another two people pulled up chairs. Conversation became general. Troy welcomed it; He didn't like the pushiness of Aida's type.

You're only interested in one woman, and she has a much more refined presentation.

He wanted to deny that interest, but Troy forced himself to acknowledge it was true.

Under cover of conversation in the group, Stacie let her gaze wander again in Troy's direction. He didn't seem interested in the gorgeous Aida. Other men were clearly smitten by the brunette's stunning looks, but not Troy.

Why hadn't he succumbed when Aida poured on her particular brand of interest? Or was he secretly interested, but waiting for the right moment to reveal that interest? As Andrew had done with Gemma.

'This was a good idea.' Troy's breath brushed her ear as he added, 'People are different outside of the work environment, and they seem a good bunch. It's halfway like off-duty time—' He broke off to answer someone's question about future plans for the plant.

Stacie was rather glad of the interruption. She needed a moment to regain her equilibrium after that feeling of his breath in her ear.

The conversation went on around them and Stacie told herself to just try to be on her guard. At least to keep her reaction to Troy from everyone else until she could get it under control for herself.

But guarded did not equate to unaware; Stacie acknowledged that when she and Troy left the pub an hour later. In the few short steps to their cars, Stacie felt Troy's presence at her side, registered every movement of his body, every breath, his body heat, the scent of his cologne.

She'd done so from the time he had stepped into the office at the plant this afternoon but, now that they were alone, all her reactions came to the surface much more strongly.

'I hope you enjoyed—'

'I think the evening without Carl there was probably a good chance for me to—'

They stopped and faced each other beside her car. In the semi-darkness beneath the street light, his face seemed to be all shadows, harshness and mystery rolled into one, and Stacie wanted to search out all of his secrets, to know him.

And she couldn't, because she'd been hurt, and her reaction this evening as she'd braced herself for Troy to return Aida's interest made it clear that she'd allowed herself to become too interested in him.

The smart thing seemed to be to get some distance from Troy. Right now!

'Well, the dogs will be hungry.' Stacie fumbled until she got her car-door open and slid into the seat, only to then look up into Troy's face and not be able to shift her gaze away.

'Yes. We should get home.' He cleared his throat. 'Each of us to our own homes, I mean.'

Not going home together, of course, although they would be driving at the same time and headed in the same direction.

Words wouldn't come so she simply started the

engine while he moved to his car, and they both got out on the open road.

His headlights followed from a distance. It was silly, but she felt oddly secure knowing he was there. There was something about Troy that simply made her feel that way. Stacie aspired to be strong, but she wasn't managing very well when it came to overcoming her attraction to him.

She was starting to wonder whether she *would* get past it, and that was about the stupidest thought she'd had since she'd believed Andrew must love her.

A jerk in the speed of her car was the only warning Stacie got before the engine cut out and the car coasted to a stop. She only just managed to get it off the road.

'What happened?' Troy drew in behind her, got out of his car and strode straight to join her as she stepped out of the vehicle.

'I don't know. I had plenty of fuel. It just stopped.' She popped the bonnet, took the torch she kept in the glove compartment and held it while they tried to look for any possible problem.

After a minute he turned to her. 'It's too dark. I think we might have to leave it until daylight.'

'The mechanic's shop won't be open again until Monday. It's probably not worth phoning roadside assistance at this hour. They'd potentially only tow it into town and leave it on the street anyway.' Stacie locked the car. 'It's been serviced recently.'

'Things happen with machinery sometimes. It's not

your fault. Let's get home; it's cold out here.' Troy led the way to his car. It was a spacious vehicle, yet for Stacie it felt like no space at all as the darkness enveloped them in their own private world and he turned the heater up to warm her.

It was probably just as well that they arrived outside her home within minutes.

'I'll see you to your door.' Troy got out of his seat before she could argue.

'Thank you.' Stacie swallowed hard before she reached for the handle of her car-door and opened it.

Troy finished that task for her, tugging the door fully open and standing there with his hand extended to help her step out.

It was just that, a hand stretched out towards her. It could have been any courteous gesture between any two people. But it was Troy, and it was Stacie's hand that fit into his as though it belonged there. It was Stacie's heartbeat that thundered suddenly as his fingers wrapped around hers.

For a moment she felt ridiculously like Cinderella stepping down from the golden coach and into a moment of magic as their gazes locked in the dim light.

'Troy?' His name was a question, and a hope she shouldn't have had. Maybe he understood that, or perhaps he simply reacted without understanding anything at all, but he did react.

His gaze linked with hers. Hooded shadows were

in his eyes, yet welcome too. Oh, she saw that, and it melted her so that when she stepped right out of the car, his hands clasped her upper arms and his head lowered towards hers, Stacie lifted her face; her eyelids drooped and she waited with an anticipation that stripped away her barriers and self-protective mechanisms.

'I don't know why...' He didn't finish the sentence. Rather, his lips lowered to hers and brushed across them in a touch that was shocking in its delicacy, a delicious, sensitive caress of lips upon lips that washed through her, drove all thought away.

Her eyelids lifted because she needed to look into his eyes. Stacie found something within the dark orbs to which she could cling, and so she did. He kissed her truly then, covered her mouth with his, and she sighed within herself as she took that kiss and gave it back.

Firm lips on hers, giving with sensuality, sipping at her lips as though he couldn't get enough of the taste of her. Her hands rose to his chest and lay flat against firm muscles as though, if she let her fingertips spread against him in this way, she could absorb more of him through that delicate touch.

Stacie didn't know why, either. She didn't know why they'd needed to do this, let themselves do this, but it had happened anyway. And, though she shouldn't, she let her head tip further back, gave herself more into Troy's hold and his kiss, and his mouth closed over hers once again.

CHAPTER FIVE

STACIE melted into Troy's arms and his touch and his kiss with so much giving that Troy struggled not to sweep her up against his chest and…

What? Carry her to her bed inside her home and make love to her through the night? It was exactly what he wanted. To want was one thing, but it also felt like what he needed—and how could that be, when Troy had made his choices? When he controlled his life and his decisions and he'd already decided that showing any interest in Stacie could only end badly?

He didn't want to hurt her, and if he had no desire to lock in to any kind of meaningful relationship he *would* hurt her. He had to stop this, now, before it went any further.

Troy was a man of discipline. That discipline had saved his life and kept his team in one piece more times than he could count. And yet right now, even as he warned himself to stop, he drew Stacie closer and wrapped his arms even more snugly around her as he kissed her again, tasted her again. He felt as though he needed that taste, needed to know every nuance of kissing her.

She brought out odd, untapped feelings in him that he didn't understand, that seemed to bypass all of his usual outlook and attitude. As he held her, he wanted to be reverent, to cherish what he held as a precious gift. New, intimidating and completely unanticipated, these concepts swelled inside him.

There'd been Linda. He'd cared for her as much as he was capable of doing. She had reciprocated those feelings to a similar degree. But theirs had been a tough, goals-focused relationship. Perfect to him, because she would not have welcomed the gentle things he couldn't give—that his mother had lamented the lack of as she'd tried to place her emotional baggage, her dissatisfaction with her marriage and her life, onto Troy.

His mum was probably still dissatisfied while she and his father roved all over Australia, part of the grey army living the retirement 'dream'.

Not your problem, Rushton. It never was.

As for all those tender feelings, was he saying he could give them now?

The question confronted him enough that he shoved it away, rejected it. He knew he couldn't give those things. He didn't have them inside him; he didn't even have what he'd given to Linda any more. He had lost his career and had to rebuild, and lost a part of himself physically as well. Troy hated the limitations that put on him.

And, if he was honest, he hated the loss of relationship and identity that he'd found in the army, a place where his lack of soft side had been a trait of value.

Was he having an identity crisis now? Was that responsible for these strange thoughts and things that seemed a lot like soft feelings as he held Stacie in his arms?

'What are we doing, Troy?' Stacie whispered the words against his lips.

What indeed? His hands were in her hair, sifting the soft tresses through his fingers.

'We're stealing a moment, and that moment is more than we should have taken.' He'd meant the words to be practical, to help back the situation off and give them both the chance to walk away without needing to make too much of it. For all he knew, Stacie hadn't and wasn't making too much of it.

But his voice was too deep. He released those straight brown tresses too slowly. His hands came to rest too gently, caressing the curves where her arms and shoulders met.

Stacie drew back at the same time he did. Her lips left his and her hands slid from his chest and down his forearms. Also slowly. Also…reluctantly.

Did she find it as difficult to let go as he did? To let her hands fully drop away, as Troy struggled to make his hands release her?

'I'm sorry, Stacie.' He didn't want to apologise for

a kiss that had been an unexpected intimacy but he had to.

'Troy, you're right. We shouldn't have done that.' She took a step back, away from him, away from what they'd just shared. A confusion of thought clouded her gaze as she, too, said what she felt had to be said. 'I can't— I made the choice to be alone. I'm not looking for a relationship. Not now. Not ever.'

'Why not? Who hurt you?'

'It's not like that.' Swift words, spoken in denial as she'd done once before.

She went on. 'My single future is important to me. The last thing—'

'The last thing we should be doing is kissing each other when neither of us is prepared to pursue where that might lead us.' Troy's tone should have been stronger, more believable. When he spoke again, he made sure that it was. 'You're right. I've made the same choice you have when it comes to relationships.'

Perhaps if he said it aloud it would help him to cement that thought inside him where it should stay. 'I don't want a relationship. I don't have the emotional…'

How could he explain the reasons? He didn't want to expose his lack to her. Why did that bother him so much with Stacie? 'I shouldn't have let that kiss happen when I knew where I stood with…romance and so on.' Troy settled for those words.

'Then we'll just forget it, Troy.' She drew a breath

and schooled her expression into an outward appearance of calm. 'I'm sure that'll be best for both of us.'

'What made you choose to be...?' Alone? What had made her decide that she didn't want to invest in a relationship?

'It was a broken relationship.' The words were tight. 'Thanks for driving me home.' She rushed on. 'I'll contact roadside assistance tomorrow morning and get things sorted out with my car.'

In her back yard, her dog let out a woof of sound. A higher-pitched yip accompanied it. Stacie turned her head in that direction before she met Troy's glance again. 'I need to go in, feed Fang and Houdini and do some things. Time's getting on, and I have a lot of work planned for this weekend.'

Work, not play. Troy had the same kind of weekend planned. It was what he should have stuck to in his thinking tonight, too. 'Good night, Stacie. I appreciated the work outing as a chance to get to know people a bit better. I've got enough of a grip on all of them now.'

The subtext was that they would both draw a line beneath what had happened here. If they both knew it, then that was how it would be.

Troy turned to go back to his car and make the small drive to his house. Distance physically, and distance mentally; if he started with that the rest would surely follow because it *wasn't* as though he were emotionally invested in Stacie or anything.

He might have experienced a couple of odd thoughts

while he was kissing her, but whatever they'd been he had them more than under control now. Of course he did. Troy put the car in gear and drove towards his home.

Stacie watched Troy get into his car and drive to his house. Once he cut the lights she went inside, took food from the fridge and outside to the dogs. Then she went about all the normal tasks she did on a Friday night.

Except Stacie kept losing track of the cleaning and sorting of laundry and other things. Her mind kept returning to a kiss that had been like no other. To a man she should not have kissed at all, but had.

Troy had made it clear he didn't want to pursue that path with her, though he'd seemed shaken by the kiss, as Stacie had been. He'd asked about her history, and she'd admitted it, but she'd wished he hadn't asked.

You're not dealing with what happened with Andrew, and you need to.

Yes, she was dealing with it. She needed to keep focusing on looking forward, not over her shoulder. Stacie did what had to be done about her place, and went to bed.

When Stacie woke the next morning, her car was parked outside her house waiting for her. There was a note explaining some technical bits of car engineering that she didn't fully understand. The bottom line was Troy had fixed the problem.

He must have got up at dawn to do that for her, and all without asking her for a car key.

In special-ops, skills like fixing cars, unlocking them and starting them without a key would have perhaps seemed every-day. To Stacie, they represented a whole other world of resilience, determination and way of doing things. One that Troy had lost.

Was that loss his reason for avoiding relationships? He'd said he didn't have the emotion; had that been drained from him as the result of his loss of career path, and of the injury that had caused that loss? Or did he believe it had never been there?

The weekend passed in separate acts of busyness at each of their homes. She saw Troy out working in his orchard. There was a lot of ladder-work involved. When he seemed to lose his footing and almost fell while Stacie was outside trimming the hedge in her front yard—which she'd been meaning to do for ages!—she almost ran to him but he regained his footing, glaring so darkly over the slip that she could sense his frustration from way over here.

Stacie went studiously back to her work. Later, when he'd gone into his gym, she left a container of home-baked cookies and a note thanking him for fixing her car.

She painted her nails lime-green, stuck fruit stickers on them and dared the dogs to say they were a silly choice. The stickers made her happy while she was sewing, so there.

Monday arrived and Carl told her they would be getting Troy in to participate in Carl's scheduled top-to-toe examination of the plant. When Troy arrived, Stacie tried to greet him normally. Had Troy spared any thought for those shared kisses since they happened?

Stacie had thought about them plenty, though she probably shouldn't have.

Troy and Carl disappeared downstairs, and Stacie tried to concentrate on her work.

'Only as I berate myself for allowing those kisses to happen in the first place.' She fanned the blank sheets of printer paper in her hands before she placed them in the empty tray.

The phone rang as Troy and Carl returned.

Stacie allowed herself one glance in Troy's direction before she picked it up. 'Tarrula almond processing plant, Stacie speaking.'

The call was for her boss; Stacie transferred it to Carl's desk.

Within moments Carl had put the call on hold.

He caught Troy's gaze and explained about the man coming through that evening, how his business could offer a substantial opportunity to the plant. 'I can't make a meeting tonight. My wife has had a minor surgery today; I'll be collecting her from hospital after work and looking after her.'

'If you need to take more time off work…' Troy began.

Carl shook his head. 'Thanks, but our daughter's

arriving from Sydney first thing tomorrow morning to spend a week with her.'

'I'm glad to hear things are working out. Stacie and I will handle tonight's dinner.' Troy made the decision and announced it firmly. Then he added, 'If you're available, Stacie? It's better to attend this kind of meeting with a strong presence for the plant, I think.'

'If it's necessary, of course I'll go.' Her heart skipped at the thought of an evening out in Troy's company but it would be all right. They had indulged in their one moment of exploration. They knew not to repeat it. Stacie certainly didn't want to repeat it—of course not. She took a breath and tried to ignore her thoughts.

'Thanks.' Troy got to his feet. 'It's not until seven-thirty, so there'll be time to go home, take care of the dogs and anything else. I'll collect you from your place.'

'I have to go, Mum. The new owner's pulling up outside in his car.' Stacie spoke the words into the phone.

'That's lovely, dear.' Mum's voice bubbled across the airwaves. 'I'm so pleased you're going on a date.'

'It's not a date, Mum. It's a work event.' Stacie bit back a stronger retort, and ignored the relief in her mother's voice at the same time.

Until Mum said, 'Before you end the call, Stacie, don't you think it's time you visited while Gemma and Andrew are here? They've news—'

'Sorry, Mum, but I really have to go.' Stacie cut her

mother off. She didn't want to hear about Andrew and Gemma. Mum was asking too much, too soon.

Stacie wanted a comfortable family relationship for everyone again, just as much as Mum must. But surely Mum realised that any hope of that was a long time into the future?

Oh, Stacie's emotions felt so torn right now.

And still there was Troy, about to drive her into town for this business dinner.

Stacie's heart-rate lifted the moment she heard Troy's car approaching outside. From that moment she battled to concentrate on her conversation with her mother. Why couldn't Stacie just view Troy as a neighbour and the man who paid her wages and let go of the rest?

Because she'd had a taste of what it could be like to be more than that to him, because she liked him, admired and was attracted to him, was curious about his life. There; was that enough to start with?

It was enough to get in a lot of trouble with—that was what. 'Bye, Mum.'

After she ended the call, Stacie threw her shoulders back. 'I'm going out there to meet Troy, to talk about business, and I'm putting every other thought out of my mind.'

With these words spoken, she checked her appearance once in the mirror in her room and hurried to the front door.

The last thing she needed was to pine over Troy. He

didn't want a relationship, and Stacie didn't either. End of story!

By the time she opened the door and walked through, Troy was halfway to it.

When he saw her, he stilled.

'Hi. I hope I didn't keep you waiting. Mum was on the phone.' *Wishing I was going on a real date with you.*

As though Stacie had any kind of hold on Troy to make such a thing happen; of course she didn't. And even if she did, and he took that up, she wouldn't want a relationship to be unevenly balanced. It should be a fair exchange, a choice that both people made because it was what they wanted.

Stacie and Troy wanted completely different things.

No, they didn't—they wanted the same thing, to live single lives. Since when had she forgot that fact about herself—even for a moment!

And she was reaching hugely even to use the word 'relationship' when it came to this man.

But in this moment Stacie registered every step she took towards him and so did Troy.

His voice was deep. Slow words seemed to rumble from his chest. 'That colour suits you, Stacie. You look…nice.' His glance dropped to peach nail-polish decorated with tiny sparkly diamond shapes, and approval shone in his gaze. 'I like your ever-changing nails. Those ones are very pretty.'

'Thank you. It's nice of you to say that.' It was the silliest thing, a validation of a quirk that her sisters used to make fun of years ago, but somehow it made Stacie feel good to hear Troy's praise.

Maybe if she hadn't caught his gaze after that, Stacie wouldn't have been as affected by the small compliment. But she looked into his eyes, and they were deep pools of admiration.

She'd teamed a pale-peach skirt and matching jacket with a pair of darker peach pumps, and had put her hair up in a loose knot held with a pearl-encrusted clip her parents had given her on her last birthday. A soft cream-coloured blouse matched the pearl clip.

'Thank you.' Stacie tried to breathe normally. 'You look good too, Troy.'

That was an understatement. He looked stunning. He had a military bearing that she doubted he would ever lose. It clung to him, or perhaps it came from within him. Tonight he wore drill trousers and a black sweater that moulded to his musculature.

You're not to notice him in that way, Stacie.

Troy opened the passenger door for her and stood back.

Stacie caught her breath, caught the scent of the cologne he wore, and fought not to close her eyes to enjoy it all the more. If she did that she'd be right back in her thoughts to being kissed by him, and she couldn't afford to think about that. She stepped blindly into the car.

During the drive they spoke of the rain, the plant, Troy's almond orchards and the number of times Houdini had found a way to be over at Troy's since Troy had first found him.

It wasn't a long trip and it passed quickly while Stacie was trying to pull her thoughts together for the evening ahead. She couldn't walk into this night overly aware of Troy. The work aspect of the evening had to be her focus.

It was raining lightly by the time they arrived outside the restaurant.

'Perhaps the weather forecast will prove accurate and we'll be rained out tonight.' Stacie spared a thought for the possibility of frizzy hair, while Troy took an umbrella from the glove compartment.

He took her arm so they could share the umbrella as they approached the welcoming lights of the restaurant. Sensible efficiency shouldn't have added to her ultra-awareness of him, but it did.

'That'll be him over there.' Troy spoke quietly and guided Stacie to a man waiting at a table set for three to the side of the room.

'Troy Rushton?' The man got to his feet.

'Yes. And let me introduce the plant's administrative assistant, Stacie Wakefield.' Troy shook their guest's hand, and introduced the man to Stacie in turn. 'Stacie, this is Marc Crane.'

Stacie smiled. 'Hello.'

Marc was an athletic looking man in his mid-thirties.

His gaze rested on her for a moment before they all took their seats.

Stacie didn't even register the attention. Well, she did, but just as a passing moment of being summed up.

And how could she even drum up enough interest to care, when the only man she could manage to think about like that was the man at her side?

Andrew had hurt her so much. She'd thought a part of her would go on loving him, even when she didn't want to. Had those feelings gone now?

She wasn't thinking of Troy in that way, of course, but she hadn't expected even to notice a man for a very long time at least.

They settled into their seats at the table. Stacie made sure she took her part in the conversation. With every moment that passed, she struggled not to fall deeper under the spell of her employer's appeal.

She'd never felt like this. It was as though, by sharing those kisses with him, she'd opened a pathway that she now couldn't seem to step off, that she wanted to follow forward.

What was she saying—that she did want to try to pursue a relationship with Troy?

Out of the question.

She'd told Troy she didn't want that, and he'd said the same right back to her.

'We don't have split shifts to work the plant around the clock, no.' Troy answered Marc's question and expanded to outline the current hours. 'Thanks to a very good manager, the plant has locked in three new almond suppliers in the past year, Marc, and we're now in negotiations with several more.' Troy continued the discussion. 'The plant shows every sign that it will definitely expand until it is running around the clock.'

'All good to hear.' The other man nodded. 'I like to understand how a plant works if I'm thinking about doing business with it.'

Their meals arrived: pumpkin ravioli for Stacie; steak dressed with sautéed prawns for the men, with herb bread in a wicker basket and crisp individual salads. Stacie ate her delicious meal and watched Troy shine as he put the plant forward in its best light to this potential business-contact.

No one would ever have known Troy hadn't been running the plant in a very hands-on fashion for years and years!

'I've enjoyed the meal.' Marc glanced at his watch and then met Troy's gaze. 'And I'm looking forward to dealing with you. I'll email you when I get back to my offices to sort out our next step.'

'I'll look forward to that.' Troy rose as Marc did.

The men shook hands and Marc left.

'He'll get soaked between here and his car.' Stacie made the observation as Marc pushed the restaurant's entry-door open and the sound of deluging rain and rushing wind met their ears.

'I suppose he will.' Troy took his seat again.

Stacie smiled. 'You did a great job of winning him over, Troy. I don't think you needed me here at all.'

'I want the plant to progress. That's just good business-sense. And don't underestimate the benefit of your presence.' Troy gestured to a waiter. As the man approached, he asked Stacie if she'd like coffee and dessert. 'It's still early.'

'I would, actually.' Stacie gave a half-embarrassed laugh. 'The tiramisu here is really spectacular.' It wouldn't be wrong to stay, to talk a little longer, just the two of them would it? If they simply spoke of work matters, didn't that mean it was fine?

'I'd rather let that rain ease off a bit before we drive back.' Troy's words seemed to decide the issue, and in a wholly pragmatic manner.

So, you see it was obvious—Troy wasn't thinking about anything even slightly close to memories of kisses. He probably had production schedules circulating in his head!

Stacie told herself she could relax, and if she felt a spark of something that rather resembled disappointment she didn't allow herself to admit it.

'You're digging in.' She hadn't really realised it until just now. 'You've taken the future of the plant to heart, not just to see it keep going, but to make the absolute best of it that you can.'

He was already doing the same with his orchards. 'You'll make your enterprises here successful, Troy. It's in your nature to make that happen.'

'No matter what the career path...' He seemed arrested by the thought. And then he looked at her. 'You're doing the same. Pushing forward.'

'Yes. I really want to make a success of the Bow-wow-tique as a full-time business, and I believe, now that I've positioned myself here at Tarrula, I'll be able to.'

He blew over the top of his coffee and sipped. 'I think you will, too.'

Will...what?

For a moment Stacie couldn't recall the thread of the conversation. She'd been distracted by lips that she'd thought from the start were made for kisses; now she knew...

'Tell me about growing up, Troy. Or life in the army. Both.' Anything to distract her from wanting his kisses again.

Too late.

And how would getting to know him more fix her problem of trying not to desire him as a man?

'I left my home at seventeen.' Troy took a spoonful of his dessert. 'I go back for visits, but my parents are retired and travelling a lot. I can't say we're particularly close. Dad's a quiet man, keeps to himself pretty much, and Mum's always found me a bit hard to...accept, I think.'

He was giving her a chance to get to know him, to glimpse his past world—where he'd come from and what made him tick.

It felt right to reciprocate, at least to a degree. 'I had a good childhood, a happy one.' Maybe that was why, as they had all got older, she hadn't wanted to notice when men started to gloss over her existence and only see her beautiful sisters.

It had taken Andrew, allowing her to believe he loved her and would eventually marry her—and then falling at Gemma's feet instead, with an engagement ring in his hand, no less—for Stacie's hopes to tumble down.

Stacie's chin came up. 'My sisters are very beautiful women.' And that was enough about that.

'Did you have a fulfilling career in the army, Troy?' Had he reached his zenith before injury had robbed him of all of that?

'I don't know if the climb ever would have ended.' The colour of Troy's eyes darkened, as he seemed to consider the question. 'But, yes, I'd reached a lot of my goals before the injury.'

He went on to explain how he'd moved through the ranks within the armed forces, into special-ops and what he'd achieved there. When Troy told her about the mission that had resulted in his injury, he was guarded about details, but told enough of a story for Stacie to realise the relief he'd felt that the mission had been a success—that no one else on the team had been injured, that they'd all got out alive and accomplished what they had set out to do.

Stacie met his gaze and something in it warned

her not to become too sentimental about all that. 'I've lived an easy life in comparison. I have supportive parents and my sisters. Now I have my farmlet to gradually bring up to standard inside and out, and my Bow-wow-tique business to grow. I'd dabbled with it for a couple of years before I moved here. I'm glad I finally got serious about it.'

'I think you've lived more than you realize, or are perhaps letting on.' His low words were observant. 'And I think I'd find it interesting to meet your family.'

Too observant; Stacie had been through pain and she didn't want to carry all of that forward into what her life was now. She wanted to leave it behind her, and he'd just hit on the one topic Stacie didn't want to explore—how she currently related to her family.

'I want to live my own life, my own way.' The words came on a burst of sound, and she turned her attention back to Troy to get away from the emotions they invoked. 'With a career like yours, would you have planned to marry?'

The moment she asked the words, she shook her head. 'Sorry. That's not really my business.'

'I was engaged to a woman who also had a career in the army.' Troy's words held a calm inflection that didn't quite seem to reach his eyes.

Somewhere in their depths, Stacie saw turbulence: anger at fate, perhaps, for robbing him of his dreams, not only in terms of work, but personally as well?

Why had the engagement ended?

'Linda couldn't move forward with me. I'd have held her back.' Troy spoke the words flatly. 'If she hadn't made that decision, I'd have made it for her.'

'She agreed to this because you were injured?' Shock made her words sharp; disapproval honed them even more. He didn't need to confirm it. The truth was in his steady gaze. 'That's wrong.'

It hadn't been love! This Linda should have been at his side, seeing him through!

A deep anger filled Stacie. Hadn't Troy faced enough, without such a loss being added at a time when he must have been able to accept it least? Yet he was saying he'd have instigated the break up if his fiancée hadn't!

'I have no emotion for a second attempt at a relationship.'

His words made it clear that he believed that he had a lack of emotion deep down within himself. Stacie had looked into his eyes; she'd seen the hardness.

But he'd held her gently, kissed her softly as well as with passion.

Had she imagined those emotions in Troy because she wanted them to be there?

Just as you did with Andrew, Stacie? Except in his case those emotions weren't truly there for you but could be found and handed to your sister.

'I understand, Troy.' In the end, she did. He wanted to be her neighbour and employer and that was all.

Whatever she felt about anything else, that was Troy's expectation.

'I wonder if the rain has eased at all?' Stacie glanced towards the door. 'We should maybe go.'

The getting-to-know you mission had certainly been accomplished. Whether the results felt particularly palatable just now or not was another thing. Well, they could be friends and colleagues, couldn't they? That was what she'd felt would be sensible from the start. Stacie got to her feet and made the choice then and there to prove they could be exactly that.

It might take all the pride and determination she had, but she would make it happen.

After all she'd been through with Andrew, she wasn't about to pine over Troy!

Troy escorted Stacie from the restaurant. He'd imparted more about himself than he'd planned to. Stacie had admitted to a broken relationship, and he'd drawn his conclusions about that: one of her sisters had stolen her man.

The hard knot in his chest must be disapproval of that sister. She'd treated Stacie badly.

Just as Linda treated you badly.

What was he thinking? Linda had done exactly what he'd expected of her.

He led Stacie through the rainy night to his four-wheel-drive. It was time to take her home and forget about swapping confidences, and too much examination of himself, when he was already quite clear just who he was!

CHAPTER SIX

'FANG won't like these high winds.' Stacie glanced towards her darkened house. She took pride in the normalcy of her tone and delivery, just a colleague who happened also to be a neighbour, making an observation about the weather as Troy drove her back to her house. 'He's not all that keen on rain, and stormy weather makes him tense unless he's inside the house with me. Hopefully it won't be upsetting Houdini either. Don't get out, Troy. There's no point both of us getting wet.'

Troy got out anyway. He took her arm to help her to the house. The wind tried to pull them over. When they got under the porch he tipped his head to the side and listened. 'That sounds like a sheet of tin flapping on your roof.'

It was hard to hear anything over the rain and he hadn't bothered with an umbrella. It would have turned inside out in an instant, anyway.

Stacie had left her porch light on. She stepped back out into the open and looked up. Even in the dark and through the rain she could make out a large piece of roof-sheeting flapping crazily.

'Come inside. We'd better see the damage,' Troy suggested. 'There's going to be a mess.'

For ten seconds as she unlocked her front door and drew a breath to deal with what she might find on the other side, Stacie heard all the doubts. Had this been a good decision? Could she really make a go of things here without this place being just a money pit?

And then she threw her shoulders back. She *hadn't* made the wrong decision. She'd made one that was what she'd wanted. She could make a wonderful home out of this farmlet, a great viable business of the Bow-wow-tique—and she would! 'I guess the roofing contractor didn't factor in weather like this when he said the rest of the work could wait.'

'Nobody could have anticipated this. Hopefully the wind won't have done too much—' Troy broke off as Stacie turned lights on inside her house.

She took one look and excused herself to change into jeans and a sweater.

'Well, technically,' Stacie said, in an attempt to be judicious as she strode towards the rear door of her home past a large puddle of water in the hallway, 'The wind hasn't done all the damage. The rain it's let through has done most of it. I've got a ladder out the back.'

I like a good challenge.

The thought whirled in Stacie's head as she carried

the ladder inside the back door. Fang was out there, of course, and barged into the house at the first opportunity, demanding at least some sympathy for the fact he'd been left to endure a wet, windy night while Stacie was out partying in town. Houdini was right on the larger dog's heels.

'I'll take the ladder. You take care of the dogs.' Troy glanced at both animals before he took the ladder from Stacie's hands.

Stacie fed the dogs and she did it fast, with a quick pat for each. By that time Troy had climbed the ladder. 'A torch would be helpful, Stace.'

Stacie already had it in her hand. She held it up and his hand closed around it, their fingers brushing lightly for a moment as he took it. It wasn't *only* that which made Stacie's heart skip a beat: Troy had called her Stace. It was just a shortening of the name; the guys at work did it all the time. But with Troy it felt different. Intimate…

'How bad is the damage up there? I should get up and look myself, Troy.' She would rather focus on immediate concerns than think about only being a friend to him.

Just as Stacie looked up and Troy glanced down, a dribble of water splashed onto her forehead and did its best to drown her left eye before tracking down the side of her nose.

'Oh!' She shook her head, blinking rapidly. Troy was descending the ladder, using the strength in the rest of his body to compensate for the limits of his shattered knee. It was an awkward descent, and halfway down his leg buckled.

'Careful.' Stacie gasped the warning and lunged forward.

'I'm fine.' He growled the words.

And he *was* fine. His reflexes were lightning-fast, and, though he still wore his dinner clothes, the shoes had a decent grip on them. He'd already caught himself, compensated. His strong arms flexed as he regained movement and completed his descent.

Oh, Troy.

How could he truly do all the work at his orchards when he had this degree of difficulty with ladders and the like?

Of course he can, Stacie. He'd get it done if that happened to him a hundred times a day, and she knew it didn't. She'd watched him often enough. Too often!

Stacie brushed the water out of her eye. 'I'm a bit concerned about fixing this loose sheeting. It's not a good time to be out on the roof.' They'd have to be creative to work out how to deal with the problem and not put themselves at risk. If they could do that, Stacie could creatively resist wanting to kiss him—and resist feeling as though all her earlier self-talk to that effect had fallen on her own deaf ears!

Now she wanted to offer a comforting hug to him as well. As if he'd welcome that right now! 'The combination of wind—'

'And rain are risky.' Troy's hands came to rest loosely on his hips. He, too, seemed to be pushing the earlier incident aside.

His frustration hadn't been directed towards her; Stacie understood that. But he had every right to feel it. She had underestimated what he must have been through emotionally thanks to his injury: the loss of his fiancée and career, as well as having to move forward and reinvent himself.

Troy went on. 'We'll have to do the work from inside the roof cavity.'

'Yes, that's what I thought.' She embraced the change of focus. She just couldn't help a sense of fellow feeling towards him at the same time. 'I'm not sure how to make that work.'

As possible solutions came to her, a wave of anticipation washed through Stacie. She'd chosen a house that needed doing up for a reason and, though a leak thanks to high winds and rain hadn't been anticipated, she wanted to fix the problem.

'Usually I'd go to my DIY books, Troy, and maybe research on the Internet if I couldn't find what I needed in the books. I have a sheet of tarpaulin, but I don't think it would be enough to fix that on from the inside. If it kept raining, the weight of the water would push through it.'

'We can fix the sheet of tin itself from inside the roof cavity without getting out on the roof—if you're happy

for me to help you? I understand
take care of everything here by you...

'But sometimes an extra set of han...
needed.' Stacie wouldn't mind his help a...
thought she would enjoy it, even if that fac... bit of
a worry!

Even so, she said, 'I'd appreciate the help.'

Troy nodded. 'We can manage a temporary measure.
It'll do until you can get your roof man out here. I have
the right tools at my place.'

Troy drove to his place to collect his tools. Stacie
had a toolbox, too, a tiered affair with matching pink
cordless-drill, screwdriver set and other items tucked
inside. By the time Troy returned she was up in the roof
cavity, had a battery-operated floodlight positioned so
they could see and her tool kit at the ready in case Troy
was missing anything they might need.

Rain pelted onto the roof; water ran through the hole
left by the flapping sheet of tin, and Stacie was in full
home-renovator mode.

'I didn't know they made tool kits in pink.' Troy's
dry words came as he joined her with a very manly set
of tools on a sensible belt fixed around his lean hips,
and a couple of other items in a bag slung over his
shoulder.

He'd changed into jeans and a jumper, and sturdier
boots.

He looked ruggedly gorgeous.

Hardly the point, is it, Stacie?

he dogs are in front of the heater in your living room. I had to dry Houdini off when we got back.' He didn't seem to notice the rough affection in his voice as he said the little dog's name. 'He slipped outside with me so I took him along for the drive.'

He gave a gruff cough. 'Stupid dog would have run around in the rain all night otherwise.'

'He seems to like your company.' And Stacie certainly didn't mind the sight of Troy looking very businesslike and ready to sort this problem out with her. She bit back an appreciative sigh. On top of that manliness, he'd just been mushy about taking care of the dog.

It wasn't fair. Just when a girl was trying to pull herself together over such temptations, Troy became even more appealing than ever. And Stacie realised that home renovations, whilst fun to do by herself, were possibly even more fun with his company.

Well, she would just take this bit of fun while it lasted, but keep it in perspective.

Stacie glanced at her pink tools and half wished she'd put pink nail-polish on, rather than peach.

'Your eyes are shining like stars right now.' Troy's low words held an edge of consciousness that he perhaps didn't realise was detectable. 'Not every woman looks forward to the thrill of fixing a leaky roof.'

'On an old doer-upper house in the middle of a windy rainstorm? No. I guess in that respect there's an inner Valkyrie there somewhere, looking for expression. One

FREE Merchandise is 'in the Cards' for you!

Dear Reader,

We're giving away FREE MERCHANDISE!

Seriously, we'd like to reward you for reading this novel by giving you **FREE MERCHANDISE** worth over **$20**. And no purchase is necessary!

You see the Jack of Hearts sticker above? Paste that sticker in the box on the Free Merchandise Voucher inside. Return the Voucher promptly...and we'll send you valuable Free Merchandise!

Thanks again for reading one of our novels—and enjoy your Free Merchandise with our compliments!

Pam Powers

Pam Powers

P.S. Look inside to see what Free Merchandise is **"in the cards"** for you!

H-R-02/12

We'd like to send you two free books to introduce you to the Harlequin® Romance series. These books are worth over $10, but they are yours to keep absolutely FREE! We'll even send you 2 wonderful surprise gifts. You can't lose!

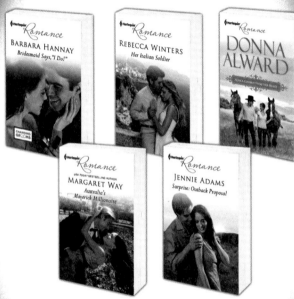

REMEMBER: Your Free Merchandise, consisting of **2 Free Books** and **2 Free Gifts**, is worth over $20.00! No purchase is necessary, so please send for your Free Merchandise today.

Plus TWO FREE GIFTS!

We'll also send you two wonderful FREE GIFTS (worth about $10), in addition to your 2 Free Harlequin® Romance books!

Visit us at:

www.ReaderService.com

YOUR FREE MERCHANDISE INCLUDES...

2 FREE Harlequin® Romance Books
AND 2 FREE Mystery Gifts

FREE MERCHANDISE VOUCHER

2 FREE BOOKS and 2 FREE GIFTS

Please send my Free Merchandise, consisting of
2 Free Books and **2 Free Mystery Gifts**.
I understand that I am under no obligation to buy
anything, as explained on the back of this card.

❏ I prefer the regular-print edition
116/316 HDL FMN5

❏ I prefer the larger-print edition
186/386 HDL FMN5

Please Print

FIRST NAME

LAST NAME

ADDRESS

APT.#   CITY

STATE/PROV.   ZIP/POSTAL CODE

NO PURCHASE NECESSARY!

▲ Detach card and mail today. No stamp needed. ▶

H-R-02/12 © 2011 HARLEQUIN ENTERPRISES LIMITED. ® and ™ are trademarks owned and used by the trademark owner and/or its licensee. Printed in the U.S.A.

The Reader Service - Here's how it works:

◄ If offer card is missing write to: The Reader Service, P.O. Box 1867, Buffalo, NY 14240-1867 or visit www.ReaderService.com ▼

BUSINESS REPLY MAIL
FIRST-CLASS MAIL   PERMIT NO. 717   BUFFALO, NY

POSTAGE WILL BE PAID BY ADDRESSEE

THE READER SERVICE
PO BOX 1867
BUFFALO NY 14240-9952

NO POSTAGE
NECESSARY
IF MAILED
IN THE
UNITED STATES

with mis-matching nail decorations, as it turns out.' She grinned. 'There's a particular kind of satisfaction in bringing something rundown back to life, even when it causes problems like this one along the way.'

Troy listened to Stacie's enthusiastic words and watched those stars dance around in her eyes. He glanced again at the pink toolbox and accepted that she wasn't going to stand back and let him fix this for her by himself.

He could have felt defensive about that. He'd expected to feel that way about dragging his busted knee up the ladder to get into the roof cavity. Yet, even with that near slide to the ground earlier, Stacie hadn't made a fuss, so Troy hadn't felt the need to care about it either.

He carried the knowledge of his limitations with him everywhere, felt it in every step. Yet now...

Well, this fix was easily within his abilities, busted knee or not. Maybe it was that certainty that ensured it didn't bother him. Or maybe it was Stacie beaming herself silly over the chance to get her hands grubby that put him in a different headspace with no relation to his physical limits at all.

'It'll be best if we take a panel of sheeting off here.' He indicated the area. 'This is about the only time that I'd be saying it's an advantage that your home doesn't have insulation batting in the roof cavity.'

'That's on the to-do list too.' Stacie moved in close

to his side to take a better look. 'How do we manage this?'

He absorbed her nearness, acknowledged an awareness of her that had deepened since he'd first met her.

Stacie Wakefield's appeal was dangerously subtle, sneaking up on a man without him fully realising what was happening.

'I'll show you step by step.'

They worked together on the repairs. The hardest work was securing the bent bit of tin back into place. For that, Troy's muscles were a necessity. By then, he and Stacie were cold and soaked again from the rain. He felt a sting on his forearm as he finally got the sheet pulled into place.

Stacie got in close beside him and worked with him to secure it. She smelled of rain, cold air and whatever shampoo she'd used on her hair, and again he struggled to think of anything but the urge to take her into his arms.

Troy allowed himself one slow inhalation before he took care of business and turned to her. 'That's done.'

'Thank you. Now I can take care of mop-up operations in the house.'

Stacie followed Troy down the ladder. She was sodden in the old jeans and sweater she'd changed into. She had dirt on her face and spider webs across one shoulder and arm. The make-up she'd worn earlier was long gone and her nails were peach and stickerless now. This was Stacie in her element. Troy wanted to kiss her until they were both senseless with it, and then start all over again.

'You've hurt yourself.' Her fingers wrapped gently around his forearm. 'I should have helped you more while you were wrestling with that loose piece of tin!'

He followed her glance and considered telling her that a bit of a scratch was nothing compared to various bumps and scrapes that had been part of his working army career let alone the damage to his knee. But she knew.

He settled on, 'Then we both might have got cut, and I'd hate to see that happen to your pretty skin.'

'Oh.' Stacie's cheeks filled with soft, warm colour and her hand stilled against his arm. She seemed silenced not only in word but in her thoughts, too.

Troy's thoughts, contrarily, were in perfect working order—thinking of things they shouldn't be thinking of.

'Come to the bathroom. We can at least clean that up before we decide whether you need to go to the hospital for a tetanus booster, stitches…' Stacie started walking.

'It won't need either.' She was fussing, but Troy followed her along the short corridor anyway, willing to humour her if it kept her happy.

The bathroom was a decent size, its plumbing elderly. Along the ledge of the deep, claw-footed bathtub was an array of bath salts, bubble baths and body washes, a sea sponge and a neck pillow.

Visions of Stacie soaking in the tub, surrounded by steam vapour, her face relaxed and filled with sensual pleasure and the room beautifully scented, flooded Troy's mind.

'I can take care of the cut at home.' That course of action suddenly seemed necessary, his self-control shaken and in threat of crumbling at any moment. God, he wanted to kiss her.

'We're here now. We might as well look at it.' Her words were practical; their breathy quality was not. Stacie was as affected by this as he was. As hungry to repeat shared kisses.

The scratch, Rushton. Let her take care of the scratch and then get the heck out of here.

Troy rolled up the sleeve of his sweater and together they bent their heads over the scrape.

'You're right. I don't think that will need stitches.' Stacie's words held relief, and other undertones that Troy *had* to ignore.

She reached for antiseptic fluid and asked questions about tetanus shots as she poured the stuff onto a cotton ball.

'I'm up to date.' He waited while she dabbed the antiseptic over the area. When she would have fumbled with the rest, he took charge and finished the job. He even made the task appear focused—no mean feat when all he could think of was pulling her close.

He'd gone halfway to indulging in pointless anger at his limitations when it had come time to fixing Stacie's roof. But in the end he'd dealt with losing his footing. It hadn't mattered, had quickly been forgotten. Had only been one moment of his knee failing him, when all was said and done.

Now all Troy could think about was the soft feel of Stacie's fingers against his arm, her down-bent head as she took on the task of cleaning up his wounds.

He drew a breath. 'It's almost worth getting hurt for this.'

'If you were a little child you'd want to be kissed—'

She broke off, unsure why she'd spoken the words aloud, but they were out there, meshed with his, each making the same statement in different ways.

'Kissed better?' Could Stacie heal him with her kisses? Heal the parts of him that had been harmed more than physically when his knee had been shattered?

As the questions registered, Troy frowned.

What rubbish were they? He'd adjusted to the injury and everything else that went with it. There was nothing more.

Right now he should move out of this room. Instead, his gaze caught Stacie's. The wish to kiss, and be kissed, passed between them. Not because of what she'd said—certainly not due to a scratch he'd barely felt.

Just because this was Troy, and this was Stacie, and when they were together that need seemed always to be there, whether either one of them wanted it to be or not.

Tonight Stacie's eyes had shone as she'd anticipated trying to fix a problem here at her house.

Something inside Troy valued the way she responded so positively to a challenge. He felt he could identify with her excitement, her enthusiasm, and with her determination to get the job done—in this case with pink tool-kit in hand.

'I'd love to know what just went through your mind.' She spoke the words as she cleared away the items she'd used to tend the graze on his arm, and they finally made their way back through the house, past the area Stacie needed to mop up.

Troy forced his feet to take him to the front door. 'I was thinking about your penchant for girly colours in dog attire, nail-polish and tool-kits. You're quirkiness, I suppose. I...like it.'

'Oh.' Her expression showed that she thought about being uncertain of herself, but it was a short battle. She grinned, then gestured towards the front door. 'I know it isn't far, but you'll drive carefully? This rain just doesn't seem to want to stop.'

Her concern was genuine and something deep inside him reacted to that. What was happening to him? Where were these feelings coming from? Because that was what they were—reactions and responses to Stacie that came from inside him and were no part of his plans. No part of him, or so he'd thought. So his mother had always told him.

He'd been a withdrawn son, happy to ignore his father as his father had ignored all of life, unwilling to buy into his mother's desire to load all of her dependence on him.

Had his mismatched parents trained Troy to lock his emotions away rather than their having been missing from his make-up, as his mum had said? And then the need to survive in army life had encouraged that behaviour. Was that the case, rather than the emotions truly not being *there* to tap into?

Troy wasn't sure what to make of these thoughts. They couldn't really make any difference to who he was anyway.

Could they?

'I'll be fine.' He asked Stacie to hold onto the dog so it didn't get out and get covered in muck or, worse, run off. Troy hated to admit it, but he seemed to have developed a bit of a soft spot for the recalcitrant animal. Perhaps he admired its determination and independent streak.

Troy now needed to obey the dictates of what shreds were left of his common sense and leave—before he simply swept Stacie up and kissed her until he'd had his fill.

Which would be never.

Their gazes clashed and Stacie drew a shaky breath.

'Goodnight, Troy. Thanks for your help tonight. I couldn't have taken care of that sheet of tin without you.'

'At least all you have left to do now is mop up inside.' He'd leave her to that. Go back to his place and let the rain drown out the need to stay with her, to draw this out for purposes he shouldn't even let himself consider.

Troy said his goodnights, disappeared through the driving rain to his car and make the short trip to his house.

'Good morning, Troy.' Stacie called the words from the front porch of her home the next day. It was still raining. Indeed the air was cold, the sky dismal and grey, and there seemed to be no sign of this weather letting up.

Yet for Stacie the sky might as well have been bursting with sunshine. She tried to put down her pleasure to anything other than what it was—a reaction to the sight of Troy drawing his car to a halt at the end of her path.

Well, she'd just have to be practical, enough so she convinced Troy she had nothing but sensible thoughts in her mind. 'Don't get out. I'll come get Houdini. I'm assuming you have him? And I have my umbrella.'

She launched forth in her gumboots with the umbrella held aloft.

Troy's face froze into a disapproving mask. He'd already had his door thrown half-open. Stacie just grinned all the more, slogged straight to his side of the car and reached in to take the dog from him. Houdini settled into her arms with a doggy sigh.

As though he'd missed her, when he'd run off to Troy's place yet again!

'You shouldn't be tromping around in this rain.' Troy's words scolded. His gaze tracked over her face and hair, lingering on the tip of her nose, before dropping to her lips and shifting abruptly back to her eyes.

She felt a sense of power that was quite inappropriate as he looked at her in that way.

And it's probably nothing more than wishful thinking. Just because he looks at you, doesn't mean he's bursting to kiss you again. If he wanted that, he would have done it last night.

'Any clue how the dog is escaping?'

'No. I still don't see where the yard is less than Houdini-proof.' It was somewhat of an oxymoron given the dog's name, of course.

Troy's mouth pulled into a dry expression. 'I thought my place was Houdini-*repellent* but he shot inside the door when I opened it anyway.'

'Maybe he preferred your company to lying in a depressive huddle with Fang, glaring at the rain.' Stacie warned herself to keep a distance, but somehow she felt she was beyond that now. She found Troy attractive. She liked him. There were things about him that called to core parts of her in ways she hadn't even begun to define as yet.

She was as hopeless as Houdini, and she truly couldn't understand how those feelings had crept in on her when she'd had so much hurt over Andrew. Over the build-up of every occasion before that when a man had ignored her for her prettier sisters, if she was completely honest.

She'd tried not to see that happening, but she hadn't been able to pretend when Andrew had dumped her for Gemma. Stacie still didn't want to go home while her sister was there, yet she missed Gemma. And she *was* becoming more and more attracted to Troy when she hadn't believed she could be attracted to a man ever again.

Troy's told you he doesn't want a relationship. That was more than enough of a deterrent, even without risking him finding someone he liked better. *You have to stay away from developing real feelings towards him, Stacie, even if they are only a strong liking.*

Well, she wasn't about to let herself fall in love with him, for goodness' sake.

'Houdini isn't the only reason I've come over. The creek is on the rise, Stacie.' Troy spoke the words into a silence she suspected might have gone on too long while she stood there daydreaming in gumboots in the rain—asking herself questions that she didn't want to think about or try to find answers for.

'There's been a decent amount of rain.' Stacie forced her thoughts to focus, even if she still couldn't entirely drag her gaze from Troy's mouth. 'Now and then the creek crosses the road, but it hasn't been a real problem.'

'In decades.' Troy nodded. His gaze lingered on her lips, before he snapped it determinedly back to her eyes. 'The real-estate agent said the same to me when I bought the farm. I guess we'll see how things go over the next day or two. It's safe for the moment. I hope it stays that way because I've ordered a hot-water service to be delivered and installed. Mine decided to chuck it in. I only realised that this morning when the water was lukewarm.'

He didn't wait for her to empathise. Instead, he said his goodbyes and left to drive back to his orchards and do what he could in the rain.

Stacie also prepared to leave for work. She'd be fine once she got there. She wasn't obsessing over Troy—and she didn't have a whole lot of irresolvable issues about family, either. She was busy. She didn't have time to worry about sorting out things that she hadn't caused in the first place. If her thoughts contradicted her desire to shove all the problems away, Stacie didn't want to know about it.

And at least she no longer had a house leaking bucket-loads of water through the roof!

CHAPTER SEVEN

TROY walked towards Stacie's home. A sense of anticipation walked with him, and there was only one reason for that: her name was Stacie Wakefield. That was something Troy had to address somehow before the vibe between him and Stacie developed any more strength.

Oh yes? Then maybe you should stop thinking twenty-four hours a day about kissing her.

In fact, he was so busy thinking about her that he didn't notice the car parked to the side of her yard until he'd already walked through her gate with Houdini at his heels. He'd made a decision about the mutt. It had been coming, and Troy had been avoiding it, but he needed to tell Stacie. He hadn't realised she would have company. Maybe it was a visitor to her Bow-wow-tique.

'Well, it's certainly been a surprise to have you both drop by like this.' It was Stacie's voice, infused with determined cheerfulness.

Troy could hear her tension from this distance.

She went on. 'Congratulations on your pregnancy. I'm happy for you of course, Gemma, and…Andrew.'

Troy frowned. What was going on? Who were these people? Why was Stacie upset and working hard to hide it? Troy had been ready to turn back. But if Stacie was struggling, he'd rather barge in and find some way to help her. He resumed his stride towards her front door.

Stacie stood on her porch with a man and an extremely beautiful woman.

'Troy. You're here.' For just a moment, relief showed in Stacie's expression—before dismay replaced it. She seemed to wrestle deep within herself, to be overwhelmed, before her chin lifted and she gestured to the couple. 'This is my sister Gemma and her fiancé, Andrew Gale. They've just shared the news of a baby on the way.'

Stacie cleared her throat. 'Gemma and Andrew, meet Troy Rushton, my—'

'Neighbour, co-worker, joint custodian of a stray pet and…friend.' Troy positioned himself at her side. He held out his hand to Andrew Gale. 'Stacie's mentioned the family.'

None of his statements was incorrect, but his tone of voice and his stance at Stacie's side suggested a degree of commitment and intimacy between them that was perhaps not exactly real. The surge of protectiveness that had driven him was plenty strong, though.

'Troy?' Stacie stiffened at his side.

He turned and met her gaze with his own steady one.

Stacie calmed from the inside out. Her body eased and leaned towards his, just the tiniest bit.

'Another busy weekend ahead again isn't it, Stace?'

'Yes.' She let her glance move about her, latched on to his words and ran with them. 'I've a lot of work to do, inside and out, and then there's everything you'll be doing at your place. And my Bow-wow-tique work.'

'We should go.' Gemma said it with an edge of relief that she tried hard to hide, and perhaps with a little surprise. 'We should have checked before we just turned up.' Her glance shifted to Troy before it returned to Stacie. 'We didn't realise you wouldn't be by yourself.'

'Yes. Perhaps phoning first would have been best.' Stacie's chest rose and fell with a deep breath. 'It was good to see you, Gemmie. You'll understand if I'm busy...'

'Yes.' Relief filled her sister's face for another reason.

Emotion crossed Stacie's—deep, grateful, torn, a little angry and hurt all at once, before she blinked and she seemed to calm a little.

'We'd best let you get on.' Gemma reached forward awkwardly to hug her sister.

Stacie returned the hug, fiercely, briefly, before letting go quickly to wave them off.

The fiancé, Andrew, drove away too quickly, the rear of his car slipping a bit before he slowed to a more sensible pace. He'd been silent throughout the exchange, but Troy had seen the discomfort in his face, the edge of guilt. So the man *should* feel guilty!

'He needs to do better than that with a baby on board.' Stacie's words were tight before she turned to face Troy. 'I can see you've worked it all out. I don't hate her. I love my sister. I just…don't really want to see too much of her at the moment.'

And they'd just driven out here to tell Stacie she was pregnant. Tight, primal instincts roared in Troy to protect her, to allow her to let whatever feelings this had raised in her out in a safe environment.

With him?

'Thank you for coming along when you did.'

Her words took him away from his thoughts.

She added, 'Gemma's very beautiful.'

If Andrew Gale had turned to the woman for that reason, Troy felt sorry for the couple, because surface looks were not what would sustain a relationship. But right now it was Stacie that Troy cared about. 'If the news of the baby…'

'Gemma seems to think—' She broke off and her expression became thoughtful, sober. 'I hope she knows what she's doing with him, that's all. I don't know how I feel about the rest. I don't think it's sunk in.'

If Troy could have healed her in that moment, he would have. 'My pride got hurt over Linda.' He understood that now, and he wanted to share it, to give this to Stacie so she would know she wasn't alone in experiencing loss. 'I know that's not the same.'

'It's as tough in its way. And you acknowledging it means you are emotionally—' She broke off as though she felt she'd said too much.

Troy didn't want to think about her words. He'd lived much of life without digging deeply on an emotional level. The idea of doing that was uncomfortable.

The pain in Stacie's eyes had receded, that was the main thing. The relief Troy felt because of that was strong. It was as though he couldn't bear for her to hurt.

She glanced down at Houdini and Fang where they sat side-by-side on the veranda. 'What are we going to do about this runaway dog, Troy? No one's claimed him and he keeps making his way to you all the time.'

It was a deliberate change of topic, and the reason Troy had come over.

'I've been thinking about that.' The fact was, Troy hadn't minded Houdini turning up so much at his place, sitting so patiently just hoping for a bit of attention or to be let in the house. Troy hadn't minded his company that much at all. 'I came over to tell you that I thought I could keep him. The back yard is secure enough. I could build a dog flap into the back door so he could get in and out of the house while I'm working. It wouldn't kill me to have him there. Besides, he'd keep pests at bay. I'm sure I caught a glimpse of a mouse the other day on the veranda.'

'Oh, Troy. That's a wonderful decision.' Stacie spoke her words of praise to Troy and blinked back the silly burst of emotion that had come with them. He'd probably tell her she was being ridiculous or something. 'And he'll be really good against rodents and things.'

'Yeah. He can yap them into running away.' Troy smiled with that quirk to one side of his mouth.

He whistled to the little dog and it rushed to his side. To Stacie he said, 'I'll let you get on with your work.'

'Yes. You need to go about your orchard work, too.'

Stacie felt surprisingly undisturbed after Troy left. She'd had so much pain over Andrew. It had been hard to hear their news without mixed emotions, but overall she truly could say she was happy for Gemma, at least in the parts of her that could give that for now.

She got hurt and it still stung, but she didn't love Andrew any more, and she still did love her sister.

Troy had made it easy for her to reach that state. He had helped her today, and she'd seen empathy in his eyes. Not pity, but understanding.

Had that understanding come from his experiences? Was Troy too perhaps changing as he adapted to the new life he was building here? Or was Stacie just trying to build castles in air because she very much wanted... what?

A chance to feel closer to Troy? She couldn't hope for that. Troy didn't want that.

And Stacie had things she wanted to achieve—by herself. That was still what she wanted.

Wasn't it?

'The creek's flooded across the road on the way to our homes. The river's rising badly on the other side of town, too.' Troy made the announcement to Stacie just before they were to leave the plant. 'I just spoke with the company that's to install my new hot-water service. They drove out to the creek and turned around again without trying to cross.'

Carl had called in with another migraine, and Troy had committed to a couple of hours just to make sure things were on track at the plant.

'That's not a joke, is it? How deep is the creek? Surely the delivery service could have driven through? I can't see how the creek could rise to an impassable level in a day. It rarely even goes over the road at all. And I've never heard of the river flooding, though I did catch a snippet on the news about the river flooding at one of the towns higher up in the state. There's been very widespread, heavy rain up there.'

More to the point, Fang was out at the farmlet; that was the immediate concern. 'I can't leave Fang by himself. You can't leave Houdini, either. We have to get back.'

'We'll drive out and see how it looks.' Troy's words were calm. 'The delivery driver said he didn't look at the metre marker. Maybe the level isn't all that bad.'

When they stopped near the flooded creek and got out of their cars, Stacie was shocked by the amount of water she saw. This was not merely a small trickle. The creek had flooded substantially across the road. The metre marker told its own story.

Troy turned to her. 'It's not actually raining right now, but that's not going to make the creek stop rising. A lot of this has to have come from upstream. The same as what's happening with the river. I know I can get my four-wheel-drive through at that water level. Your car's a bit of a dicier prospect. I'd recommend leaving it on this side.'

'I think that's wise.' Stacie gathered her things, locked her car and walked the short distance to Troy's with him. 'I'm mostly concerned to get to Fang. I don't want him to be isolated out here.'

Troy hesitated with his hand on the keys in his ignition. 'Would you prefer me to drive you straight back in to town once you get your dog? I'm comfortable that I can get us through even if it rises up another foot, but you could stay in town until we're sure the creek's on the way down just in case.'

'No. I don't want to...'

Leave Troy out here by himself.

It was so silly—it wasn't as though he couldn't look after himself—but that was how Stacie felt. She drew a breath and tried for a more normal tone. 'If there are worries about being able to get in to town to go to work, that will change things, of course. For now, I'd rather be in my own home, if you're happy with that.'

'I am. Let's deal with tonight, for starters, and see how things are in the morning.' Troy drove them through the water, driving carefully to compensate for the tug of the current, and tapping the brakes several times once he got out.

'That wasn't so bad,' Stacie said optimistically, and wondered just how much the creek would go on rising. Surely it wouldn't rise much more, and in a couple of days would recede off the road completely?

As she had that thought, she saw the water lying all about her home. Sheets of it covered the front garden, the path and were pushing far too close to the veranda. 'That's not from the creek.'

'No. There's been a dump of rain here earlier in the day, by the looks of it.' Troy's gaze shifted from her home to his.

'At least there's no water lying around over at your place, Troy,' Stacie added judiciously. 'Well, there are a few puddles.' She let her gaze return to her own yard. 'This is a problem, though. I'll have to dig a drain to shift the water away from the house.'

'*We'll* dig a drain.' When she would have argued that he'd done more than enough work for her already, Troy held up a hand. 'You can always trade me a hot shower for the work.'

'Oh.' She hadn't thought of the implications of his hot-water service not being delivered. Now visions of

Troy standing under her shower with water running down his back and chest pushed their way into her mind. For a moment Stacie forgot where she was, what the problem was. All she could see before her and in her imagination was Troy.

How could she be that way? Shouldn't she be fixating over seeing Andrew Gale again? And the pregnancy?

But Stacie simply didn't care about Andrew any more. She doubted she would ever like the man again, but she was over him. That fact was now abundantly clear to her.

And do you truly think it would be that easy to push thoughts of him aside if he'd really mattered to you that much in the first place, Stacie?

The question sobered her. She *had* fallen in love with Andrew.

At least, she'd felt sure she had, and it had hurt when she realised he'd maybe never really been as serious about her as he'd let her believe. What did this mean? That she could still feel hurt about that, but not truly care about Andrew himself, and desire Troy all at the same time?

It meant that Stacie's capacity to over-think things and make herself crazy in the process was too well-developed!

Stacie threw her door open and stepped out into her soggy yard. 'You can use my shower for as long as you need to, Troy.' She'd just work somewhere else in the house while he did that. Or take a walk outside. Or something.

'Thanks.' He searched her gaze for a moment and nodded. 'So, do you have shovels?'

'I've got one shovel and one spade.' She let her sense of humour peek out. 'Bought from a clearing sale at dirt-cheap prices.'

His laugh was short, but deep and rich. 'I'll go get a second shovel.' The smile faded. 'I want you to wear gloves. I don't want you coming out of this with blisters on your hands.'

Stacie hadn't heard him laugh like that. It was a sound she could get used to. 'I'll guard against blisters. Bring Houdini over. He can be company for Fang while we dig the ditch. I'd better go inside and put a pair of jeans on to go with the gumboots I'm going to need for this.'

Did Troy give a quiet groan before he turned his head away? Stacie couldn't be sure, but for some reason her pulse rate was suddenly faster, stronger. Despite the dismal weather, the water everywhere and the sky still looking grey and sodden and likely to dump further wet contents all over them at any time, she suddenly felt quite cheerful.

An hour later Stacie perhaps felt a little less enthusiastic. Her lower back was letting her know that a term of Zumba classes earlier this year and taking Fang for regular walks apparently hadn't put all her muscles in perfect order for this kind of task.

They were digging through a patch of ground that seemed to be nothing but water and red clay. She'd taken the gloves off minutes ago so she could keep a better grip on the shovel but she knew she wouldn't last long without them. 'I thought this farmlet was all sand.'

'There's different ground depending on where you look. My farm is the same.' Troy glanced up from his work. He had boots on his feet that looked as though they'd have kept him in good stead during his army days. His jeans were wet and covered in muck to the knees.

Stacie tried to focus on practicalities rather than the temptation to let her gaze shift upwards to his firm chest, to each feature of his face.

Troy had cast more than an occasional glance at her, too. An awareness hummed between them, but she was happy. In this moment—and somehow thanks to that first visit with Gemma even if she had brought Andrew along—Stacie felt happy. More hopeful. She'd thought about there being a little niece or nephew, too. Maybe that would feel more real once Gemma started to show a baby bump. Stacie would love it, though. She acknowledged that thought fiercely.

Stacie picked up her pace, digging with determination and tossing the mud aside as she went along. Was she trying to dig herself out of the danger of how Troy made her feel?

She didn't know how the accident happened. One

moment they were both digging, while Stacie told herself she wasn't thinking about Troy or wasn't casting
glances his way every chance she got, the next her feet
slipped from under her and she went flying towards
him. There was a split second to realise she was going
down and might potentially hurt him on the way. She
gave a shocked squawk of sound, had the good sense
to toss the shovel and then Troy's hands were reaching
for her.

'I've got you.'

'No, Troy, don't!'

But it was too late. He caught her and her momentum
carried them both down, Troy rolling to protect her fall
as they landed.

They rolled again. Stacie felt the wet slick of mud
coating her. Water splashed up and then they lay there,
two very mucky people in some very cold water and
slithery mud. She'd ended on her back with Troy poised
half on top of her.

'Tell me that landing didn't hurt your knee.' Her
hands held his hips.

'It didn't.' His voice was low and deep. 'Tell me I
made sure you didn't get hurt on the way down.'

'Does hurt pride count, for being silly enough to fall
over in this?' She meant it as a joke and he seemed to
know that, even with the breathy quality of the words.

Stacie was fighting consciousness of their closeness,
but she lost.

Troy's body was firm and blanketing over hers. His

chest pressed against the softness of her breasts, and there was no denying what their closeness had done to him. He wanted her, and Stacie wanted to arch against him…

'God, Stacie.' His hips pressed once against hers and then he seemed to force himself to stillness.

Every fibre of her being longed for him in that moment. Stacie had never felt this way, had never felt such intensity of longing that seemed to come from deep within.

His face softened and his gaze wandered over her hair and face. His arms were locked about her, holding her safe where their bodies pressed together. His warm heat contrasted with the coldness beneath her.

'It wasn't your fault.' He spoke in a husky tone, a hungry tone. 'You slipped.'

Shivers went down Stacie's spine, delicious, delightful shivers. 'And now we're both a mess. My hair's got mud in it.'

She had to force the words out, an attempt at calm when she was anything but.

His gaze consumed her. Passion filled his eyes, seemed to tighten every sinew and muscle in his body.

They were locked together and both trying very hard not to acknowledge the white-hot flare of desire.

Troy shifted slightly above her. A clump of mud fell from his ear and landed on her cheek.

She stifled back a laugh. The intensity was not lost, but the mood gently changed.

'Go ahead and laugh, Stacie.' He spoke in a low tone that was playfully stern. The lift of one side of his mouth negated any idea that he was actually annoyed. 'You know you're equally covered in it.'

'I'm sure women pay hundreds of dollars for a beauty treatment just like this.' She felt proud of the quip, even if it was breathless.

'It reminds me more of mud wrestling.' His fingers brushed the mud from her cheek.

She drew a breath, inhaling the scent of mud and Troy's skin. 'I guess you're used to dealing with nature's extremes.'

'Yes, but not…like this. God, Stacie, is there any way that you wouldn't appeal to me?' He bent his head and pressed the lightest of kisses to her brow, the tip of her nose. He even kissed her cheek beside where the mud had landed.

She thought they'd avoided this, that they'd turned their corner, but they hadn't. She'd been fooling herself because that was all it took—that one press of his lips to her skin. Stacie cupped the back of his neck and drew his lips to hers. She kissed him. She took what she wanted and gave what she wanted to give, and as his lips responded to hers, she thought, *I want this, and he wants it*.

His lips were cold. Hers were too. Passion warmed them, warmed Stacie's blood, made her even more conscious of Troy, of the press of his body, even as he shifted to his side and held her in his arms, held her up out of the mud that had coated both of them. One broad hand stroked between her shoulder blades and down, through the mud slicked over her sweater.

The touch was sensual, primal, seemed to speak of his strength and power. And Stacie loved it.

When he looked into her eyes and pressed kisses against her lips, she couldn't look away, couldn't think of anything except this. Couldn't react to anything but his touch, his scent and his mouth on hers.

'It's dangerous.' The words slipped from her, a fear spoken aloud—because it wasn't only her senses that responded when he held her, that seemed to open up to him and let him close, and closer still.

Affection; it was affection, not deep emotion.

That wasn't so bad.

And desire. Of course it was also desire.

And you really, really like him as a person—more and more as you get to know him.

But the affection, the desire, the liking, all felt as nothing she had felt before. Not towards Andrew, not towards any other man.

And to Stacie, who needed so much to feel safe and in control of her life, her destiny, her world, that knowledge was frightening.

It still wasn't a problem. She told herself this, insisted on this. Because she wasn't falling for him. And he certainly wouldn't be falling for her.

He wouldn't. She had to remember that.

'You're right. It's dangerous.' Troy released her. He got to his feet and held out his hand.

Stacie took that hand and let him draw her up. She brushed muddy hands down mud-caked, water-soaked jeans and forced herself to reach once more for the shovel. She wanted to go inside, to avoid this, not to let her thoughts run forward any more. But she couldn't do that. And it was better to behave as though this was nothing. 'I'll take care not to slip again while we finish this.'

The words were double-edged, just like the shovel in her hands.

She set to work for the second time.

CHAPTER EIGHT

'I GOT a change of clothes and scraped enough of the mud off this lot so I wouldn't track it through your place.' Troy barely registered his own words.

All he could see was Stacie, fresh from her shower, hair still wet against her shoulders in a slick fall. All he could think of was holding her in his arms in the mud, kissing her with nothing but the elements surrounding them.

'It wouldn't have mattered. The living room's the only one with carpet in it, and having Fang around means I mop the house pretty much every day anyway. At least, I do in this weather.' Stacie stopped and bit her lip as though she felt she might be babbling. 'I do hope that creek doesn't get us stuck out here. We need to be able to move around.'

So they could avoid being aware of each other. Did she really think it would be that simple? The thought wasn't helpful but it came to Troy anyway.

Resistance, Rushton. You have the self-control for this. Use it.

Yeah. He'd used it really well while he'd kissed Stacie in the mud.

They'd finished the ditch. Stacie had obviously taken care of Fang while he had been gone as well, because the larger dog had been waiting in front of the fire in the living room when Troy walked inside with Houdini tucked under his arm, sniffing him madly trying to work out why Troy smelled and felt the way he did.

At least Troy had broken Stacie's fall so she didn't hurt herself. He tried to convince himself that was the highlight of that event.

He failed. Failed even more as he looked at her in yet another pair of form-fitting jeans and a fluffy sweater. His glance dropped to her feet and it was his turn to smirk. 'Nice slippers.'

She followed his glance downwards, and pink stole into her cheeks. 'I was going to change those before you got here.'

'Oh, I don't know. Bunny slippers as big as small boats are probably all the rage at the moment.' It showed Fang's good training if the dog resisted the temptation to chew on those, Troy thought. Whereas Troy just wanted to take them off her...

One-track mind, Troy.

'I'll go shower.' Announce it, match action to words. Get some distance and forget how good she felt and how sweet her lips were, even in a setting of muddy ground. In any circumstances.

'There's a clean towel for you on the railing in the

bathroom. I figured you'd bring anything else you needed.' Stacie's glance shifted to the toiletries bag in his right hand. 'And of course you have, because you'd be very good at being prepared.' She snapped her teeth together before prising them apart enough to add, 'I'll sort out dinner for us both. I have stew in the slow cooker, so I'll thicken it, and it will be ready by the time you've had your shower.'

Sitting across a table from her, sharing a meal again: insanity. 'Thank you. That'd be nice.'

Troy made his way to the bathroom.

'Troy, I was just—'

Trying to get to her cordless phone, ringing from wherever she'd left it—her bedroom, by the sounds of it.

'Do you want me to get—?' The rest of Troy's question went unasked. He just tugged the bathroom door open and stepped out—shirtless and wearing clean jeans.

A fact Stacie discovered when she rushed straight into him and her hands came to rest on his warm, damp chest. His skin smelled of something male and appealing that he'd dabbed on there or washed with. Stacie drew a sharp breath and fought the urge to swoon.

Swoon, for crying out loud. Just like a woman of yesteryear.

She got no further than that thought before his gaze locked with hers and he drew a sharp breath. In the back of her thoughts, she noted that her phone had stopped ringing.

Somehow his hands were in her hair and her head was tipped back. He didn't bend her to his will; Stacie gave herself to his hold with a trust that she didn't fully understand.

It wasn't like their previous kisses. With those there had been awareness that they were testing new ground, even as they believed that ground should not be tested.

Now Stacie met Troy's mouth with hers and kissed him with everything inside her that she'd held back, with parts of her she hadn't even known needed expression. Let alone that Troy was the one to bring out that expression.

Why? Why was he the one? What did that mean?

How could she hope to find answers when all she could do was experience his touch? His taste? Kissing him to a depth that she had never looked for in such an exchange before—not with any man she'd known.

Out in the mud, she'd thought there couldn't be more than that experience, those kisses. Now there was, and she was out of her depth with no capacity to run or hide. Yet, even as she thought it, she knew she wouldn't choose to do that anyway. She wanted this.

'Stacie.' Troy's mouth opened over hers. Their tongues touched, tasted.

Her fingers spread across his chest.

His hands sifted through her wet hair as though he'd

never touched anything so appealing, so enticing. As though he wanted to hold on for ever, kiss her for ever, and never stop this.

Could they keep going?

Should they?

Before the questions fully formed, Stacie pressed closer and his arms tightened about her.

Which came first—her move to be closer to him? Or his to hold her closer? It didn't matter. Nothing mattered except his touch, and her touch, the sharing of this and how much it ministered to a welling of need inside her that covered so much more than simply a need for closeness.

Stacie needed to be close with Troy, to be kissed by Troy, to kiss him in return and feel the press of their bodies against each other. To learn each angle and plane and store the knowledge into a memory bank inside her, but that was only the start.

She needed to know him, everything about him. His hopes, dreams, opinions, thoughts and feelings.

Towards her? It was a question that she didn't want to acknowledge because to do that was to say she cared deeply for him, and hoped for the same in return—she couldn't, and he wouldn't.

'Kiss me again, Troy.' She whispered the words against his lips, an abandonment to the moment and a yielding of herself that moved beyond any decisions she had made or any questions in her head.

He looked into her eyes. Maybe he searched for

answers. Maybe, like her, he was looking for something that came from within himself that he had to understand and currently didn't. Whatever it was, his gaze deepened and his hand cupped her cheek, her chin, before he lowered his lips and ravished her with rich, sweet kisses.

Those kisses led to more kisses, the press of bodies to more closeness until she could no longer define herself. She was part of him and he was part of her. She wanted to make that closeness a completion in the most intimate way there was.

That thought, that urge within Stacie, was so strong and came so deeply from her emotions that her eyes widened and she felt as though something inside her had changed and realigned. She wasn't the same any more and it was because of Troy. Because of how he made her feel.

'It's all right, Stace.' His hand brushed over her hair, soothing now rather than caressing. Giving rather than taking and exchanging.

'It's never been like this for me.' The words were a whisper. She wasn't sure even if she had said them out loud.

But Troy said the words out loud. Earlier, when they had talked about all of this and they had agreed that neither of them wanted the complication, neither had been looking for a bond, a relationship. Not that sort.

Neighbours and work colleagues didn't equate to

intimate kisses that could have taken them straight to the bedroom. 'I'm—'

'Don't.' He said the single word and released her as he did. Held her at arm's length and then dropped his hands completely. 'Don't apologise for something that we did together. I don't know why it's like this for me with you. I know my boundaries, my choices, and yet…'

Yet when it came to this his self-control slipped. Somehow, acknowledging that gave Stacie the control that she needed. She drew a deep breath, pasted on the most normal expression she could muster and pushed aside what they'd just shared.

Later she might draw it out and think about it—indeed, she knew she would have to—but for now she stepped back into the role of neighbour and a little bit of colleague. 'I don't know who was trying to phone, but if it was urgent I'm sure they'll try again. Other than that, dinner is all but ready to serve, and I do hope you'll still join me before you go home to attend to things over there.'

'I will.' Troy let his gaze rove over Stacie's face and then wondered if he should have done that.

She was flushed from their kisses, her lips soft and swollen. In her eyes was the gentleness that was at the core of her, all of her strength, her determination to pull this back from the brink and return it to an acceptable working relationship for them.

That seemed a joke now.

Troy wanted more of Stacie than he had the right to ask for or that she wanted to give. And he wanted to give more of himself. Not in the kind of meaningless exchange that could happen between a man and a woman, but...differently.

He still felt protective of her. In fact, during the visit from Andrew Gale and Stacie's sister, that protectiveness towards Stacie had filled Troy, making it hard for him to even communicate normally with the couple.

Stacie had handled herself during that visit. She was handling herself now, too. What Troy wasn't handling was the fact that he seemed to be thinking of her as 'his'. His to care for, to try to protect. How had that happened when he knew it couldn't happen? He couldn't be forming some kind of real and deep attachment to her.

He forced himself into guest mode, finished getting dressed then sat down to dinner at Stacie's table once again.

They simply would have to persevere and find some normality again.

That had to be possible.

CHAPTER NINE

'No, Houdini!' Stacie shouted as she and Fang stood on the home side of the swollen creek two days later.

Splash.

The little dog hit the water, went under, resurfaced and was immediately swept along by the current. Stacie ran to the edge. Fang was at her heels.

Troy heard and saw all of it in a few brief seconds as he pulled his car to a halt behind them.

'Hold!' Troy shouted the word like the commanding officer he'd once been. He threw his car-door wide and ran to Stacie's side. He didn't think about his damaged knee, he simply compensated and he got to Stacie as fast as he could.

'Troy, Houdini's gone in. He won't be able to fight the current with the creek so swollen. He'll drown.'

Already the small dog was being swept down-stream.

'I came out looking for him. He must have followed you and Fang. The creek's deep here and the current's strong thanks to all the rain again yesterday and last night. The river's to the brim outside of town too. You're not to go in, Stacie.' No options, no negotiation.

Stacie might or might not have considered jumping in. Troy was making the decision for her. He glanced about him and spotted a large fallen branch. He strode towards it. 'Go to safer ground. Take Fang with you.'

If Houdini couldn't or wouldn't swim to Troy's branch once he got it in the water, he'd have to go in after the dog himself, and he would. He could handle the water and these conditions. He didn't know if Stacie could.

Houdini turned his head and saw them, and tried to swim against the current to get back, letting out a whine as he struggled. The little dog's head went under once, and then again.

In a few short seconds as Troy dragged the branch towards the water's edge, Fang broke away from Stacie's hold and leaped into the water, landing well out and swimming strongly towards the smaller dog.

He got Houdini by the scruff, lifting his head above water level and paddling to get back to the bank.

It was a struggle for the larger dog. He, too, went under once as he battled with the weight of the smaller dog held between his strong jaws.

'Oh my God.' Stacie's words were whispered. 'I can't believe Fang's doing this. He won't make it. There's no way.'

'I agree.' Troy tossed the branch aside and waded into the water. He was chest deep and fighting to stay upright in the current when Fang got to him. The dog wasn't giving up its bundle, so Troy took the pair of them into his arms and slogged towards the bank. The current tugged at his legs and he stumbled once, almost going down thanks to his weak knee before he reached the bank.

'Troy! Be careful! Don't drown!' Stacie again looked ready to leap into the water.

'We're all right. I've got them both.' Troy started to climb out.

Stacie held out her hands.

Fang wriggled.

Troy released him and the dog struggled to his owner, dumping the bedraggled Houdini at her feet before he proceeded to shake himself. He shoved at the smaller dog with his snout.

Houdini was sodden, dazed and scared. From the look on her face, Stacie was equally as shaken. She petted both dogs, she looked Houdini and Fang over, and she cast worried glances in Troy's direction during those few seconds of time.

Houdini shook himself and seemed to regain some of his equilibrium.

'He's okay. See? Your dog saved him.' Troy hoped the calm words would help Stacie.

Both dogs moved away from the water, trotting back towards the house and no doubt the warmth that they both wanted right now.

'Are you okay, Troy?' Stacie rushed to Troy. She all

but dragged him the few final steps out of the water. 'I thought you were going to lose your balance and fall. I know you're strong, but I was worried!'

She patted her hands over his arms, chest, neck and face.

Troy bore it rather well, he felt. In fact, it was quite nice to be fussed over by Stacie. She was worried about him and stressed out because of what had almost happened to his dog, and potentially hers. 'I was prepared to go in after Houdini. Fang beat me to it. I was more concerned about what might happen to him once he jumped in. He means a lot to you.'

'He's not the only one who matters to me.' She was still patting, fussing, muttering words about him getting too cold and how his knee would hold up to such rough treatment. That she should have jumped into the water herself before Fang went in—and how had Houdini got there anyway, he hadn't been with Stacie when she had set out.

'That last is a rhetorical question, I'm assuming.' Troy interrupted her fussing flow to murmur the words. Her first statement, he tucked away in a safe place inside. He wasn't sure if Stacie even realised what she'd said.

The depth of his voice gave away what it meant to him to know that she cared, to hear her put it into words, and that was something Troy needed to think about. 'Houdini loves the challenge of escaping. He didn't love this particular escapade, though, so maybe he'll think twice before he does anything quite that risky next time.'

He caught Stacie's hands in his to still them. They came to rest clasped in his, against his chest, and Troy felt pleased. He wasn't letting her go. Not yet.

Not this time.

A moment passed between them. Stacie's gaze locked to his, Troy unwilling to look away. It seemed right to clasp one of those hands in his to lead her to his car. 'Let's go back. The dogs are probably already there.'

'You have to get dried off, too, Troy.' Her fingers curled around his hand as though by holding on she could take charge of everything. Keep him safe. Look after him.

She didn't have to convince him to do what she asked right now. All she needed to do was look at him. He wanted to please her, to give her what she wanted or felt she needed, even if she was fussing over him.

Not emotionally involved, huh, Troy?

Well, he wasn't emotionally invested. Not in that way. He was humouring Stacie's needs right now, that was all.

All except for the desire inside him to draw her close, to kiss her worries away and go on kissing her. That wasn't a 'Stacie' need. That was a 'Troy' need…

Rather than going home to Stacie's, both dogs had headed for Troy's front door. Perhaps Fang had felt the ongoing need to keep an eye on the smaller dog. Troy brought towels from the outdoor laundry-room and they dried the dogs off.

When Troy opened the door to the house, Houdini shot inside. Fang followed. 'They've gone to the living room. The slow-combustion wood fire's on in there.'

Did the words sound normal? Troy didn't feel that way. He wanted Stacie in his arms, wanted to hold her, take away the residual concern from her expression. Troy wanted to possess her but, deeper than that, he felt that he *needed* to. Every event from when they had first met seemed to have been leading to this. Inexplicably. Inexorably. Inevitably.

'I was going to see about bathing them.' Stacie frowned. 'But maybe we should just let them dry out there first and worry about the rest later. You should take a shower, though…' She stopped and chewed her lip and her face flushed in a beautiful bloom of consciousness.

Troy cleared his throat. 'At least I managed to cobble the hot-water service together enough that it's working for the time being so I can take a hot shower here.'

'Yes, that's a good thing.' Her words were a little breathy as they stepped into his home.

It was her first time here, and Troy liked the look of his house with Stacie in it. He liked it a lot.

'You've made it nice in here, Troy.' She let her gaze rove the area.

'I plan to be here for a long time.' They stood in the

front hallway. The dining room and kitchen were to the right, with a large living room to the left.

And a bathroom down the hallway with the promise of a hot shower in it. Troy shucked out of his wet sweater and shirt and tossed them back out the front door. They landed with a wet plop that brought Stacie's gaze to him.

She didn't move, didn't draw a breath. Her expression barely changed but, oh, it changed so much to reflect every spec of desire Troy felt towards her, right back to him in return.

It was that change that had Troy's pulse racing. She was still pale. It had been cold out by the creek and she didn't have a coat on, just another soft sweater and a pair of those stunning jeans that she didn't seem to realise were stunning.

Stacie began to stutter. 'You—I—that is—' She shivered.

She needed to get warm. Troy needed to get warm. And they both needed each other.

'Will you run the shower for me?' The words emerged in a low, deep tone. They were a question and an invitation and an admission of need, all rolled into one. The first two he understood. The third he would admit to himself because he always tried to deal honestly.

She read it all in his eyes. The invitation, the offer to retreat, and perhaps the need that even now he tried so hard to deny.

Maybe she understood, too, that him asking her to run the shower was a long way from being any kind of order or instruction. It was a need for her wrapped up in a man's few words.

He hoped she would see and understand the rest from within herself.

She searched his face for a long moment. He waited. Whatever was in his eyes, he made no attempt to shield. After a pause, she gave a slight dip of her head.

When she turned and walked ahead of him, further into the house towards the open door of the bathroom at the end of the hallway, relief swamped Troy for a moment.

He would have the chance to express to her in actions the things he couldn't put into words...

What did he mean by that? The question faded away as he stepped into the bathroom behind her. He thought of another moment, a different bathroom. The gentleness and need for gentleness that he'd sensed in her then. What was he doing?

'I want this to be right for you, Stacie. I don't want you to regret it later.' When it was over. When this led to whatever it led to.

Would that be to an ending? Or to the beginning of an interlude between them that they could both enjoy in a mature way until they agreed to put a stop to it?

The questions registered, but dimly, because other questions filled his mind.

What if I can't make it right enough for you?

That was the strongest and it came from somewhere deep inside where Troy believed there was a lack of softness, inability to be tender enough, to find enough of that side within his nature. He might have left the army, but the personality that had made him good at his work there had not left him.

Could he find those emotions? Did he have them, if he dug deep enough?

'It will be right for me, Troy.' Her belief in that was in each word, in her movements as she turned on the taps in the shower and as she turned and raised her hands to his chest.

That touch...

Troy closed his eyes and felt it somehow deep inside. And he knew that in this moment, in this encounter, he would give all that he had, and that he would take this. He wouldn't stop it, now that he was sure it was what she wanted.

With reverent hands he lifted her sweater and let it drop to the floor behind them. The bra she wore was crimson silk trimmed with a darker crimson lace. He might have known she would choose something pretty and bright, with her love of fabrics, but Troy felt as though he'd learned something new about her, another piece of information to tuck away.

The touch of her hands on his chest felt like heaven, or perhaps the closest to it that he would ever get.

'You'll shower with me?'

'Yes. I need the warmth. You do, too.' Her words

were about being out in the cold. About Troy wading into a river and getting soaked, her worry about the safety of two dogs and one man.

But the words were about so much more than that. Even if Stacie didn't realise it right now, she'd named feelings, something within each of them that believed they could find that warmth by being together. A well of tension rose in Troy's throat because he didn't want to feel exposed in that way—yet when it came to Stacie he was.

And he was taking this because beyond that unease was all that they could share together. Here. Now.

'I will do all that I can and give all that I have to give, to bring you that warmth.' That was his commitment. He helped her remove the rest of her garments and shucked out of his remaining clothes. He'd seen her once already with her hair wet. Standing her under the warm spray and making it that way again now was a gift.

Each plane and angle of her face was revealed in all its beauty. Water turned her eyelashes into spiky clumps and dampened her cheeks. He kissed her mouth as they stood under the spray, kissed petal-soft lips that bloomed to his ministrations until he had to stop kissing her and pay attention to learning other parts of her and encouraging her to learn him too.

They washed and soaped each other standing beneath the hot water, cocooned in this world of just the two of them while elsewhere in the house two dogs ignored them, uncaring of anything but themselves and a warm fire.

Stacie looked at the scarring around his knee, just looked. She already knew its impact on his life. That was where the real scarring remained—in the things Troy couldn't do.

The thought registered, made him frown, because there was something in it.

'Turn your back.' Her instruction was soft, almost a whisper.

Thoughts drifted away as Troy turned and felt the ministration of soapy hands learning him by touch, even as he learned Stacie's touch upon him and knew he'd never forget it.

He didn't tell her she was beautiful with flowery words or phrases. Troy was not good at those words.

Instead, he committed his efforts to showing her the truth of her appeal. Each touch of his hands carried that message. Each time he looked at her, he revered what he saw. When the shower was off and they were dry, he took her hand and led her to his bedroom, shut them inside in a haven of privacy and quiet where he could focus on pleasing her, giving to her with all that he had.

Troy was her opposite. He couldn't give all to Stacie that she deserved to have. But, what he had, he would give generously and open-handedly and at least she would know that.

It seemed as though time stretched out. That was

what Stacie thought as Troy laid her on the bed and came to her, giving her slow, sweet kisses as she found her way through final layers of shyness to receive all of this interlude with him. This wasn't new to her, but in a way it was because she felt so differently with Troy, and so much more deeply.

'Stacie.' He said her name.

Just that, and yet in that moment she felt as though she had all of him, everything he had to give to her. The overwhelming thought came and was kissed away as his mouth covered hers, and he brought them together finally. Stacie forgot all but Troy. Just Troy, just this sharing.

Would it lead to more? Stacie couldn't control that hope. It was part of bringing this to Troy, of sharing this with him. For all her efforts to protect herself, she couldn't seem to do that with him: she could only give and want to continue to give.

And to receive, as Troy kissed her and encouraged her. Finally, when it was time, he brought their closeness to fruition in a way that somehow made her know she was utterly safe with him, that all they shared was meaningful and good and right.

She found the warmth she had looked for, and she kept it as Troy wrapped his arms around her and they lay quietly as their breathing slowed.

Troy tugged the covers about Stacie's shoulders, allowed his hand to trail once from her shoulder blades to the base of her spine before he simply wrapped her close in his embrace once again, released a long, slow exhale and then matched his breathing to her slower cadence.

He wouldn't sleep, not in these moments that were for him to cherish. Troy wanted to mark each one by the breaths that she took, to hold her until she woke naturally. He did that, and when she woke they made love again slowly, looking into each other's eyes.

'I need to go, Troy.' She emerged from his bathroom. She was fully dressed.

Troy had pulled on jeans and a thick sweater, put boots on his feet and attended to the dogs so it would be easy for her to go when she was ready.

Now she was, he didn't want to let her go, but he needed the time because this had been so much more than he could have anticipated: holding her. Lying with her wrapped in his arms. Waiting until she'd fallen asleep and then stroking his fingers gently over her face, committing the feel of her soft skin to his memory while she wouldn't know how much he needed to do it.

'If you want anything—' He stopped himself. 'Whatever you need, Stacie.'

'Time.' She bit her lip before she went on. 'I need time to understand.'

What had happened, what their sharing had meant. It was what he could benefit from, too, though Troy wasn't entirely certain he'd be able to figure out answers. How had this happened when he'd thought he understood everything? Maybe in that passage of time it wouldn't feel quite so strong, startling and overwhelming as it did right now. 'Take what you need, Stacie.'

'I'm going to have an open house for the Bow-wow-tique in a couple of weeks, if the creek recedes and my yard dries out enough. I really should sew for that.' Her words revealed her confusion, her need to think, to find understanding. 'That's how I'll probably spend my weekend.' Stacie called Fang to her and left to walk the short distance to her home.

Would she find that comprehension? If so, where would it take them? Or where would it not?

CHAPTER TEN

'IT'LL be all right, Fang. I'll get all the work done and have enough stock prepared before the first dog-show is held at Tarrula at the end of next month.' Stacie murmured the words to her pet where he sat stoically at her feet in her Bow-wow-tique room. She lifted a piece of quilted fabric into her hands, laid the biased edging over it and began to pin it in place.

Before she returned to work on Monday, she wanted a satisfying pile of completed outfits. The online sales were increasing, and her first open day was just weeks away. Each effort brought her a step closer to realising her dream for her Bow-wow-tique.

Stacie pushed aside all thoughts that she might not be able to get to work due to the flooded creek, that her home might be waterlogged when it came time for the open house.

Troy had encouraged her efforts with her business.

She couldn't push that thought away, either, couldn't stop her thoughts straying to him again and again. He hadn't been out of her consciousness since they had made love last night. Since she had woken hours later, made her excuses and gone home.

He'd insisted on walking her, a man, a little dog, a girl and her muscle-dog walking through the dark, wet weather to her home so close to his home.

'I have so much to do this weekend, Troy.' That was what she'd said. But inside, she'd been thinking, *I'm overwhelmed. I don't know how I could have let this happen. I've never experienced anything so beautiful and special in my life and I don't know how to even start dealing with how it's made me feel.*

Stacie pulled the remaining pins aside and put her foot down on the sewing-machine pedal. Sewing her way free of the thoughts.

But Troy was there. Every nuance of his face, every moment in his arms.

No matter how she tried not to let it happen, her thoughts circled back to him. Stacie pursed her lips and sewed harder, and when that didn't work she stopped sewing altogether.

All right, they'd made love last night—beautiful, passionate love that had left Stacie fulfilled, shaken and overwhelmed because that fulfilment had seemed to come from so deep in her heart.

Had that just been her? How had Troy felt? What had their night together meant to him? No answers came. She'd known they wouldn't come. Whether she stopped to think, or tried *not* to think, her confusion and feeling of being overwhelmed remained the same.

She finished sewing the dog-coat and went to the cupboard to sort through her fabrics. But somewhere inside Stacie wanted to make her way straight back to Troy's house and just walk into his arms and…stay there.

'It's not possible!' As Stacie spoke, Fang jumped to his feet and trotted out of the room, tail wagging.

A visitor? One that Fang knew and whom Stacie hadn't heard arrive. Troy…

Even as she heard the knock on the door, her heart started to pound. She wasn't ready—not to see him again, to confront what they'd shared, to try to understand her feelings about it and figure out what to do about those feelings.

'I know you're probably working, Stacie.' Troy stood on the other side of her door with Houdini at his feet.

The weather behind them was grey and dull. Behind Stacie she had dog-clothes patterns spread across her kitchen table, chairs and fabrics all through the living room.

'The creek's started to recede.' Troy's hand rose to the back of his neck. 'I thought you'd want to know.'

As he spoke, a gust of bitter wind blew through the opened door. Troy's gaze searched her face.

Stacie pushed the door properly open. 'Thanks for telling me about the creek.' Before she got any further, Houdini shot into the house.

Troy's gaze followed the little dog's movements until Houdini disappeared from sight inside the house. Even then, he didn't quite meet Stacie's gaze. 'May I come in for a minute?'

'Of course. I'll make hot drinks.' Just like a good hostess would.

Stacie wanted to be that, but what would they talk about? Would Troy want to speak of…?

'I'm in the process of creating a production line.' She gestured to the chaos in the living room and on her kitchen table and chairs, scooped fabric off one of the chairs and gestured for him to sit there. 'I have to get a lot of garments made.'

The jug boiled while she had her back turned to Troy. She pulled down cups from a cupboard, coffee granules, sugar, and milk from the fridge.

'Let me do it,' he said quietly from beside her.

She stared at the coffee jar. The lid was threaded crookedly. How long might she have stood there, fussing with it, putting off the moment she would have to turn and face Troy?

Now that moment had come. She handed over the coffee jar; they shared one glance and Stacie had to accept that her world truly had changed.

It had changed when she'd rested in Troy's arms and felt the touch of his fingertips stroking over the curve of her shoulder as he'd held her. When he brought her to completion—and not only her body, but also her emotions embraced him.

'Stacie…'

Was Troy trying to figure this all out, as she was?

Or had what they shared been no more to him than any other encounter?

'What comes next, Troy?' The question emerged even as she warned herself to avoid the topic.

Well, that wasn't going to be possible, was it? He was here to confront this very thing, to say whatever needed to be said. Because after last night, after today, they would still be neighbours; she would still work at the plant he owned. Houdini would still adore Fang's company. Stacie would still look out her window and glimpse Troy working in his orchards.

'I don't know if I can do this.' The whispered words came straight from her heart, straight out of the pain she'd experienced when Andrew had fallen in love with Gemma and Stacie had felt ashamed and lost—thrown out as though she didn't really matter, just because her sister was beautiful and Stacie…was Stacie.

But that was all over now. Stacie didn't love Andrew any more, so it didn't matter, did it?

No, you don't love Andrew, because you've fallen in love with Troy instead!

That couldn't have happened! It would be a disaster if that had happened. Troy—yes, *Troy*—didn't want it.

She was imagining that reaction within herself. That had to be it.

'I…wanted to speak to you about last night.' Troy's words were hesitant. He took a sip of his coffee and then set it down. His hands clasped his knees and it was as though with that touch he held onto all the confusion that Stacie carried inside herself. 'I don't understand—last night—how that was between us…'

'I don't either.' It was a relief to admit it, but didn't that just make it worse?

'I've never felt that way with a woman, Stacie.' The words seemed wrenched from him.

She knew then that it had meant more to him than just something to be forgotten afterwards. She'd thought it at the time, but she'd been afraid to believe it.

It was dangerous to believe. Why did she have to care so much? It was impossible to think without the risk of every thought being imprinted on her face for him to see.

She couldn't love him. She couldn't, couldn't, couldn't!

She didn't know what to say. She wanted to protect herself. 'I haven't, either, but Troy…'

What did she say? That it mustn't happen again? He was probably here to tell her exactly that. And yet the thought of never being in his arms again, never kissing him, holding him, sharing touch with him…

From the moment she met Troy he'd been in her thoughts. She'd wondered about him, wanted to get to know him, and as they had settled in as neighbours with each other she'd come to know him—and with each step of knowing…

He'd rescued her when Gemma and Andrew had visited, and Stacie had thought she was just grateful for Troy's input, even somewhat embarrassed that he'd worked out the situation. But he'd stepped into that situation determined to help her.

And she had loved him for it. Loved him for reluctantly making friends with a little stray dog, too, and for helping a girl fix a roof in the middle of the night when he didn't have to do that.

For limping into her life and being frustrated that his life wasn't perfect, that he'd suffered losses too, but determined to make a go of it anyway. He'd done that, even when he'd lost his army roots and all that it must have meant to him. He'd lost a fiancée into that bargain. Stacie had admired him and somehow, without realising it, she'd found strength within herself by knowing him.

The strength to fall for him.

'Stacie. Are you all right?' His deep words held concern, care for her, and willingness to blame himself swiftly and fully if she was hurting.

When he went on, his words only confirmed that fact. 'If I've made you uncomfortable...'

'I am, but not that way.' How could she regret what they'd shared? She searched his face, realised how dear it had become to her, each feature. She had held him, stroked her fingers over his cheeks, nose, mouth and forehead.

He'd done the same and in his touch there had been tenderness, giving, and in what they had shared an emotional connection that defied either of their understanding.

Don't imagine he felt that way, just because you did.

But you are in love with him, Stacie. Deeply, utterly, all the way in love with him, and there's no going back from that.

She felt elated, shocked, amazed. Stunned. And terrified. Oh, so scared. That she would love Troy, love him with all her heart, with such depth of herself that she looked at him and she had to fight and hope that her feelings weren't visible on her face.

She'd done something that she'd promised herself she would never, ever do again and had invested her heart and emotions in a man.

Yet it was so different from how she'd felt about Andrew. That now felt like some weak, shadowy impression of love. These feelings for Troy filled her. How could she have missed this onslaught, allowed it to fully form within her before she stopped it?

How could she stop it now? Yet she had to. She couldn't risk this. Troy himself had said he didn't want that kind of involvement.

'I'm all right, Troy.' The words were husky and nowhere near convincing enough. She cleared her throat, tried to pull herself together, to come up with words to convince him.

Of what? That their love-making hadn't changed her life? Because in the end it had. They'd made love, and Stacie had slipped so gently over the line all the way into love with him that she hadn't realised it had happened.

How could she trust any man to commit to loving her, and not be swayed or distracted when someone prettier, smarter or more appealing came along? Or when he decided he didn't want to be in love after all?

Troy had already made that decision.

'It's all right, Troy. Truly.' She drew a breath, forced words to form and emerge in a coherent way, in a way that just had to convince him. 'We shared a special night together. You don't have to apologise for that happening. I'd be sorry if you did because I valued it. What we shared…'

'Was special.' He seemed to search for words, to feel as out of his depth as she did.

But not for the same reasons.

Troy drew a breath. They weren't touching. They stood in her kitchen, drinks poured, the ritual dispensed with, but neither of them cared about it. His gaze flickered over her face, caressed as though it were a touch, before he seemed to pull himself up, seemed shocked perhaps by his own reaction. 'I'm not a man made for a girl like you, Stacie. I had my one chance at that, and when I became injured—'

'Was she very beautiful, Troy?' Was that why Troy couldn't settle for someone so obviously outshone by her sister, by both her sisters? Though Troy had not yet met Angie.

'Linda? I suppose so.' He seemed to brush the question off as though it were irrelevant. 'She didn't want a highly emotional relationship, and that was why we suited, until the changes in my career-path ended that.'

Stacie tried to listen, tried to hear with her mind, not her heart—because it was full of love for him and already hurting, because it was so clear this couldn't work, that she was on her own in those feelings. He didn't share them. He didn't want to and, even if she had tried to fight them off, they'd caught her without her permission.

Troy would have been caught, too, if love was meant to be between them. Stacie wouldn't call herself a romantic. She'd been against the idea of ever committing to a man again! But she believed that much.

'It's not about Linda, Stacie.' Troy led the way to the kitchen table, cleared another chair and waited for her to sit on it before he sat at the end of the table, facing her.

Their knees could bump; that was the ridiculous thought that went through Stacie's mind as she sat. She could bump knees with him.

She craved his touch. Even now, as she fought herself, she craved the chance to step into his hold again, to express all that was inside her for him. 'I know it's not about Linda. It's about a night we shared that mustn't be repeated.'

Because, if it was, Stacie would only fall even more deeply in love with him and then it would be harder still to go forward. 'We don't suit, you and I. We make good neighbours, and you're a good boss, but you have your limits as a man and I have mine.'

'You're right.'

He agreed so quickly, with such conviction, that it was difficult not to feel humiliation.

And yet in the back of his eyes there was something she couldn't define that made her pause—that looked as far from a rejection of her as it could be. That looked… hurt? But his words…

She was clutching at straws, hoping he would care for her in a way that he didn't.

'There'll be awkwardness, Stacie, but I want us to overcome it.'

He went on, forcing past the feeling that she was rejecting him for the same reason Linda had ended it. 'I don't understand why I allowed such a loss of self-control, but you can rest assured it won't happen again. We can go on as before knowing that I don't have any desire…'

You do. You do still desire me.

She wanted to say it and make him agree to it, wanted to force him to admit what she was certain she'd seen in his eyes. There was at least some attraction to her still within him.

Well, apparently, if there was he wanted to crush it as quickly as he could! Humiliation tried to cut through her where it had sliced its way in the past. This time she had to be stronger. She had to.

Stacie tipped up her chin and forced her gaze to

return to beautiful pieces of padded cloth and trims, buckles, straps and bindings. 'I appreciate you coming over to speak to me about this, Troy. I'd have come to see you if you hadn't done that.'

She didn't know if she would have or not, but it was best to say it. Even if the words hurt, Stacie would finish all of them. 'I want to value you as a friend.'

'I'll still help you with any DIY projects you have, if you want me to.' His lips twisted in an almost bitter line. 'Anything I'm capable of.'

She didn't understand why he'd even passed that negative comment! He was certainly capable of every-thing any other person could achieve, even if it was through sheer bloody-mindedness and taxing on his physical abilities. That determination was one of the things she loved about him. 'I need some time, Troy, to come to terms.' With how she felt about him, and how she was supposed to manage those feelings when she didn't know how to end them or even try to get them under better control.

Irony rose in her thoughts and she spoke before she could censor them. 'I need to see my sister, go home and visit while she and Andrew are there. I'm going to be an aunt. I'd like to sew for the baby, be comfortable around Gemma again.'

Troy frowned. 'If that's what you need, but he hurt you.'

And now Troy had hurt her a great deal more, but he hadn't meant to. He hadn't done anything that Stacie hadn't fully wanted and embraced. It was just that their love-making had released the love inside her for him and he couldn't and didn't return that. 'Maybe Andrew just trained me to be stronger, and to recognise when I'm better off by myself.'

'I understand, Stacie. It's what I thought, too.' Though Troy had come here to say exactly these things to Stacie, he had to work to force the words out as he agreed with her. It was just that Stacie had had her say too, and she'd let him know that she wasn't prepared to stretch to try to be with someone who had his limitations physically. He'd told her he couldn't give to her emotionally. Maybe he'd misunderstood the rest.

What does it matter, Rushton? The end result is the same. You know you're no good for her. That's how it is. The words had to be said. She agreed with them. It's easiest for both of you now because you've agreed on your terms.

That should fix everything.

So why did Troy feel as though the bottom had just fallen out of his world when, aside from being his neighbour and someone who worked at the plant he owned, Stacie had no other impact on his world?

No? Then why did he think of her all the time? Why had holding her in his arms and receiving the gift of intimacy from her felt so special, so amazing? Why had it opened a yawning place inside his chest that seemed hungry to be filled and yet which Troy had no idea how to fill?

Troy didn't have the answers. All he knew what to do was give her the emotional space she'd asked for. He ought to know how to give that. After all, it was what was lacking in *him* that meant he could never be all that she needed!

CHAPTER ELEVEN

'THE situation is out of hand.'

'I can assure you, as Mayor of Tarrula—'

'Take a look around you, Mayor. It doesn't matter what you have to say, or even whether you're willing to roll up your sleeves and lend a personal hand. If we don't get this levee bank in place a lot faster than is happening, the whole town will be under water before nightfall!'

It was Friday morning of the following week. Steady rain through the week had pushed the river to the brink of its banks. Now, massive rains overnight that had managed to escape the predictions of the weather bureau had forced the water over the top.

The floods weren't critical.

Yet.

But there was a lot more water coming.

Troy's gaze narrowed as he examined the area. Stacie stood at his side. That was a whole other state of emergency that Troy needed to deal with because walking away from her, ruling a line under what they'd shared and saying it mustn't happen again, wasn't working for him.

He missed her. Though he saw her across the way each day—had been in to the plant on several occasions and spoken to her there, had visited with Houdini as he and Stacie pretended all was well, helped her shift trestle tables around in her back room to create more space for her Bow-wow-tique work—all was not well.

They were going through motions of normalcy and neighbourliness that weren't there, trying to create them to cover their true feelings.

Somewhere deep inside, Troy felt as though it had come alive after lying unacknowledged and ignored for much of his life. He needed to think about that, to try to understand what those feelings meant.

'This is terrible, Troy,' Stacie whispered beside him. 'If they can't get a levee bank to hold the river back, the plant will go under. You could lose everything.'

'You're right. I can't be polite about this any longer.' He raised his voice. 'Every business in the town with manual labourers and hardy men stops work now.' Troy spoke the words with a calm authority that came straight out of his army training. He limped to the mayor's side. They'd spoken earlier in the week; the mayor had been disinclined to heed Troy's warnings or listen to his suggestions then. He'd felt things wouldn't reach critical point. The town hadn't suffered this kind of flood in almost a hundred years, after all.

Troy went on. 'We work non-stop bagging. Levee

bank first, then businesses. What's the time frame to evacuate homes?'

The mayor frowned and blustered. 'Well, I—'

'There's no time for this, Mayor. You want this situation under control. I have the training to make that happen.' Troy rapped the words out. The crowd had fallen silent. At least they were listening. 'Time frame?'

'One p.m. today.' The older man seemed to deflate.

'Then let's get moving.' Troy rapped out his orders. The men were already there and hit the ground running.

'What can I do, Troy?' Stacie had made her way to his side. Now she touched his arm briefly.

Troy felt that one touch as though he soaked it in through the pores of his skin, a drink of life to a dry well inside him. 'Stacie...'

She waited, her expression showing her confidence that he would know how to direct her. They had a crisis on their hands. Anything else would have to wait. 'Go to the plant. Get Gary to shut the work down. Don't worry about what product gets left mid-process. Just get all the men over here.'

Stacie rushed to do Troy's bidding. He'd held back at first from taking control of the situation with the sandbagging. But there was so much flooding going on across four states of the country that the SES and the armed forces were stretched beyond their limits trying to cope with it.

Tarrula was small. The workers were needed to levee the larger town upstream of them. The people of Tarrula had been told to get out; the SES and local police would be supervising that evacuation. But that was only if it had to happen. If the town could get enough levee bank built in time, then at least some of the homes wouldn't have to evacuate, some of the businesses would not get flooded, and overall the flooding would be a great deal less. They had to try!

Across the next three hours, Stacie watched as Troy marshalled troops and got things moving. He was on his feet, moving about, speaking to various people and getting the sandbagging efforts streamlined. When there was no more organising to do, Troy rolled up his sleeves. He was a strong man, slowed by the awkwardness of his damaged knee but certainly not stopped by it.

Stacie pitched in too, and at the end of three hours, with everyone working together, they'd got their levee bank very close to finished.

'It's going to work out, Troy. By minutes, but it will work.'

'Yes.' The one word emerged, and Troy turned to glance at her. Maybe he twisted his bad knee or it failed. He stumbled down from where he'd been working atop a final pile of sandbags, tossing them closer so men could pick them up and place them on the levee.

'Troy!' Stacie jolted forward, but another man had already grabbed Troy's arm and steadied him.

'Let me finish it, boss.' A moment later that man had replaced Troy on the pile of bags.

The mayor hurried to Troy's side. 'We've made it. Couldn't have done it without you, Rushton.' He pumped Troy's hand.

The tension on Troy's face was not all about the impending flood crisis. He'd hated that near fall, and being assisted when it had happened. Stacie knew it, and she wished she could comfort him.

'We'll go back to the plant now, make sure it's secured before the river peaks.' He said the words emotionlessly to Stacie and then said his goodbyes to the mayor before starting for his car.

Stacie nodded and followed him, and tried not to think too much about the myriad emotions crowding through her right now, but they came anyway.

Pride in Troy's achievement, gratitude that the town would escape being flooded thanks to the efforts that Troy had coordinated when the mayor hadn't had the kind of strong presence needed to get people working in a coherent whole.

'You did a great job out there.' Stacie spoke as they stepped into the factory. Other workers were close behind them, all streaming in to do Troy's bidding now that the sandbagging of the levee bank was taken care of.

Troy turned and looked at her. His eyes were stony. 'I got things organised because the mayor wasn't going to get that done. Anyone not prone to panic could have done what I did, and a lot more physical labour to go with it!'

His tone warned her not to say more, warned of the bitterness at his physical limitations that went a lot deeper than she had realised.

Oh, Troy. Don't you know how special you are? How little that physical restriction matters to me? Only because it hurts you.

She could have felt brushed off by that stony look, even hurt by it. Beyond the stoniness lay anger at his injury, and yet he did so much and did it well and she wished he could see that.

'Let's get this plant locked down in case the worst happens.' Most of that work was already done. Troy supervised the rest, and before Stacie knew it she was back in his truck for them to make their way out to their homes.

'The creek's risen a bit more again.' Stacie made the observation as Troy drove his truck through it. 'It's hard to believe it's only two in the afternoon. I feel exhausted already. Thanks for getting me safely home, Troy.'

They'd stocked up at the grocery store before they had left town. Stacie glanced behind her. 'I think we're ready for a month-long siege with that lot.'

'We probably won't need it, and will hopefully be cleared to get the plant back up and running by the end of the week.' Troy finally met her gaze, and his softened as it took in her windblown hair, the muddy patches on her clothes and her general state of disarray. 'You're a trooper, Stacie. You might be small, but—'

'I'm a dynamo with a sandbag? You did a great deal more than me today.'

They'd stopped outside her house.

He got out of the truck and started unloading her bags of groceries. 'I've been happy to see you more yourself today. At least there's that.'

He limped past Fang, onto Stacie's front veranda and dumped bags of groceries there before turning back to retrieve the rest from his truck.

'Thanks for bringing those.' Stacie was slightly breathless as Troy walked into her kitchen with the last of her groceries. She quickly put away the perishables, and then walked back to the door with Fang at her heels. 'I'd rather ride over with you than walk. It's a bit muddy.'

Before Troy could do more than raise his eyebrows, because he hadn't exactly invited her, she walked through her front door with her dog and waited for Troy to follow before she closed and locked it. This man needed some sorting out. And Stacie was going to try to do it!

Stacie had a militant, determined expression on her face. Troy looked into her eyes, looked at features that were familiar to him now. He remembered touching her face with his fingertips and…he longed.

For her touch. To kiss her. To hold her close and not let go until he'd had his fill of holding her.

When would you have had enough, Rushton?

'I can take care of my stuff by myself.'

She glared at him. 'Well, I know that, but you helped me.' She let her dog into the back of his truck and climbed into the passenger seat, folding her hands in her lap and waiting in prim, grubby determination for him to drive the short distance to his home.

Troy drove. He didn't understand her determination to stay with him, and she clearly thought he was so decrepit that he needed her help to carry the remaining groceries.

'That's quite a frown you have going there.'

Her quiet words made him realise he'd driven to his house and not got out from behind the wheel of the truck. His hands were gripped around it and his jaw was clenched.

He wanted to say, *I'm not an invalid. I can do as much work as any man.* Troy had approached his injury with that view in mind. But there'd been times, working his orchards, when he'd had difficulties thanks to his knee. There were times when that knee let him down. 'I can handle the groceries,' he repeated.

'I can't handle where I am emotionally at the moment. There. I've been honest about it.' She drew a breath that shook just a little at the end of it. 'If we're to find some way to be neighbours and friends as we were before, then I need to spend time with you in that capacity so I thought this would be a way.'

To do that. Not to feel sorry for some broken-down

man, but to help them to heal and be more normal with each other because she needed that.

'You can bring the lighter bags for me.' He glanced at her. 'And deal with Houdini's excitement when he sees his visitors.' His gaze softened. 'Maybe a coffee after that. You can tell me how your boutique sewing is coming along.'

Whatever she needed. That was what he'd said to her, and he'd been so busy conducting his personal self-pity party that he'd almost missed those needs.

You need more than that from her.

The thought demanded acknowledgement. Before he could give it, Stacie blew out that deep breath, threw her door open and climbed out.

She reached for the first two bags of groceries. 'That's a good plan.'

They hadn't talked since Troy had seen her the morning after they made love, not in any serious or meaningful way. Maybe that was what had left Troy feeling so vulnerable. And even confused.

Where were his crystal-clear instincts now? His ability to assess situations, make instant judgements and know that he'd summed things up correctly?

They brought in the groceries. Stacie fussed over Houdini and the two dogs parked themselves in the living room in front of Troy's heater.

Troy made coffee and brought it to Stacie, and when he eased into his chair tried not to show that his knee was hurting.

'Am I keeping you from a hot shower, Troy? Or anything else?' Stacie put her coffee-cup down and sat forward where she'd taken her seat on the lounge at his side.

'Getting off the leg for a bit will do the trick.' He knew his body and his limits. What he hadn't understood was the depth of the sense of loss. 'I can't ever get it back, Stacie—that perfect physical condition.'

Stacie hadn't wanted to be burdened by it, yet she was so kind in her thoughts and actions when it came to that. That didn't make sense; he frowned. 'You can't accept that about me—the loss of physical strength in that respect.' Maybe if he said it aloud, he would figure out how to understand it.

'Are you crazy?' The words burst out of her, and the expression on her face as she searched his matched them for shock and denial. 'I would never take such a view of you, even if you were limited—and in your case, well, that's not even how it is!'

Was she in delusion land? Trying to console him and not finding the right words?

Or had he misunderstood in the first place, leapt to an erroneous conclusion out of his own uncertainty? 'You mean that, don't you?'

'Of course I do, Troy. I've never known anyone as resourceful, strong and determined as you are.' She swallowed and seemed to be looking inside herself too as she went on. 'You might have a physical challenge that you have to deal with, but you deal with it. What you achieve in life is exceptional. Anything you set out to do, you do and you make a great job of it. This morning, organising everyone.'

'I did that because the mayor couldn't control them and not enough was getting done.' He hadn't wanted to step in, to make it seem as though he felt the mayor was incapable of getting things together, but in the end expediency had won out. Troy hadn't been willing to suffer major damage to his factory if there wasn't an unavoidable reason for it. 'I fell off the damned pile of sandbags!'

It was the first time ever that he had admitted to such humiliation instead of stomping on it, ignoring it, pretending it didn't happen or in some other way avoiding it.

Of all the responses he could have imagined Stacie giving, she said, 'Technically you didn't fall.' She paused to examine a purple nail that was rather the worse for wear from their morning's activities. 'You lost your footing when your knee gave out, and one of the others grabbed your arm and stabilised you until you got your footing back. Did it really feel like a big deal to you? Because it didn't look like one. Any person could have had the same experience up there.'

Troy stared at her. He thought about being offended by her casual words but of course they weren't really casual—they were thought-out and measured, and they put him and his sorry-for-himself attitude very neatly in place!

He gave one short, low laugh. 'You'd make a great person to have around to stop a man from getting on his high horse.'

She smiled. 'Or stressing out if he fell off it?'

He sobered. 'I thought you had a problem with that.' When she didn't seem to understand, he went on. 'About me. That it was why you felt you couldn't consider exploring anything more with me after that first night—my physical limits.'

'No, Troy. It was nothing like that.' The smile disappeared from her face and her expression softened.

For once, though she might have wished otherwise, there was no guard there. Just a vulnerable girl who looked at him with confusion and longing in her eyes, and other emotions that Troy wasn't sure he could define.

He took her hand. He didn't know what made him do it, just that it seemed as though he had to. Once he had her fingers held in his palm, Troy searched her eyes again.

Stacie looked back. She seemed so raw, so vulnerable, and yet she'd pushed her way in here today so she could force him to accept himself.

What about Stacie?

What about how wonderful *she* was, and how worthy of every good thing that could come her way, and of being completely proud of who she was?

It hit him, then, what all this had been about for him: the protective instincts towards her, his hope that she would be able to make a full-time living out of her business. The need that he had felt and been unable to define when he had asked her to stay with him, when they had made love. All those things had been leading to this realisation, this crystallisation of every sense and emotion.

He was in love with her.

That was what had happened to him. Yet how could this be? How could he have fallen for Stacie, fallen in love with her in this way?

Troy had believed himself incapable of such depth of emotion. He realised now that it had all been waiting, locked inside him, until the right woman came along with the key.

But what could he do about this? Did these feelings truly alter anything? They altered his outlook, his mindset, the parameters of his hopes and needs.

But could they alter what was ahead for Troy and for Stacie? Could there be a 'them'? If Stacie truly hadn't rejected him because of his physical limitations—and knowing her as he did he shouldn't have assumed she would do such a thing—then what had she meant by those words she'd spoken that morning?

How could he find a way forward when he didn't know how Stacie felt about him other than her concerns about committing? Were these feelings even real? Could he encourage Stacie to reach out, to love him? Was that even possible?

So does that mean you simply do nothing and hope

she'll develop feelings for you somehow without you making any effort whatsoever? Or you assume yours will go away?

Troy might have a busted knee but he was a man of action. There had to be some way that he could pursue this. And the feelings wouldn't go away; deep inside, he knew that. His mother had been so wrong.

'I've seen who you are now, Troy.' Stacie spoke quietly into his silence. 'The way you took charge in town today. You self-assess, and you do what has to be done.'

'I've always done that in a hard school. Today was about that, about protecting my interests.' But it had also been about the community, protecting all of it.

'You're a just man, Troy. You took charge today for the sake of everyone.'

He dipped his head because he had to acknowledge it. 'It's true. But how does that…?'

She drew a breath. 'When you received your injury, I know that you'd have put achieving the mission before that injury no matter how threatening it might have been. You have some loss of physical ability now, some restriction on what you can do, but you're honourable, Troy. You're completely honourable, and I just don't believe that a man can be that way and be emotionally detached in the way you've said that you feel you are, and would be in, in a relationship!'

She'd struggled to get the words out, and in the midst of his doubts and the knowledge that he'd fallen in love with her hope flared inside Troy. If Stacie cared about this to such a degree, then surely she must want to try to find a way for them?

Yeah? And what made him think there could *be* a way? Or that Stacie could truly embrace a future with him?

'Troy, I need to tell you—'

'Stacie—'

They both stopped, but Troy needed to speak this, to tell her what was inside him. Even if she couldn't accept it, *he* needed to accept it.

'I didn't understand what happened to me, the night we made love.' That had been the start of it, of him realising. 'You were special from the first day I met you. I knew that, but I didn't understand why. I know you've been hurt, Stacie, and I don't want to be responsible for hurting you again. I feel that I may already have done that.'

'Because we made love and you had to walk away from that afterwards.' She shrugged her shoulders as though it didn't matter, but the lie of that was all over her face, in the grip of her fingers around his where he still held her.

That hold felt right. Troy stroked her fingers and that, too, felt right. He said, 'I walked away because I thought if we…went on in that direction you'd get very hurt.'

'You wanted to protect me. I understand that.'

The softening of her voice told him she appreciated his care.

But that wasn't all of it. Somehow he had to explain the rest, tell her that he loved her—if she rejected that offering, deal with it.

Yes. His soldier's training wrapped around his instincts and emotions and the decision was made. It was worth the risk!

'I did need to protect you.' That instinct had been in Troy, not only because that was what he did, but because of Stacie. 'At the time, I didn't think I could give you what you deserved in life.'

'What do you mean, Troy?' She whispered the words. 'I don't understand.'

Troy understood, but it wasn't easy to put the feelings into words that would seem so inadequate. He pursed his lips and did his best. 'I'd scale a mountain for you on my hands and knees. I'd watch over you, make sure you stayed safe. If hard decisions had to be made for your sake, I'd make them and act on them, and I wouldn't look back.'

That was his army training, and it was the core of him that had made his choice of that vocation work so well for him. But there was more. 'I'd do those things for anyone if they were necessary, Stacie, but I'd do them for you simply because I could, or if you'd let me, or if you told me you needed them. You... No one has mattered to me the way that you do.'

'I pushed you away.' Her words were low. 'After we

shared that night together and I felt feelings for you so deeply and didn't know—I was afraid of getting hurt.'

'Because your sister and Andrew hurt you.' Troy searched her eyes. He wanted to take her into his arms and tell her that none of that mattered. That he would never let anyone hurt her again.

But she needed to get this out, to release it. And he needed to hear it so he could figure out how to help her let it go.

'It wasn't only that.' Stacie's shoulders tightened. She seemed to consider her words before she finally went on. 'You've met Gemma. You've seen how beautiful she is.'

Troy frowned. 'That's irrelevant.'

'Wait.' Stacie's fingers squeezed Troy's' hand. She could barely believe they were here, talking about this as though there were a chance that they might find a way forward into—what?

She didn't know, but there were things here that had been misunderstood, and if sorting them out could even make the slightest difference, or give them half a chance, then she wanted that half-chance. And she had to admit to Troy how she had felt in the past. There was trust in that, and self-confrontation, because she had never really fully acknowledged all these feelings from life growing up with her two beautiful older sisters.

'My sisters are both older than me, so I grew up in their shadows anyway.' She hadn't minded. 'We had a good, loving relationship between us, and in the whole family, too. It's still there somewhere. It just got a bit tense and buried under…other things.'

'When your sister stole Andrew from you.' Troy's face could have been carved in stone, and yet Stacie could feel so much that was far from stony emanating from him.

She'd learned to read him, to see beyond that façade to what was going on underneath. 'You're angry on my behalf.' That moved her. She loved him for it.

Was there any chance at all that Troy could love her in response? 'That situation happened more than once. There were other men who started out interested in me, and lost interest very quickly the moment they set eyes on my sisters. I guess I was a sort of Cinderella in reverse. My sisters were the beautiful ones and I—'

'Be very careful what you say.' His jaw locked. 'I've never met anyone who resembles that analogy less.'

She heard his abrupt words, but she couldn't fully take them in. Now that she'd started, she had to go on.

'Guys did that, and I didn't mind too much because I'd never really had any serious boyfriends, so I wasn't too upset if that happened.' Also, her sisters had turned their backs on that sort of behaviour, and Stacie had appreciated that. 'Andrew was different. He let me believe we were serious, that there would be a future. Then he turned to Gemma, and she…'

'Tell me, Stacie. It's better to get it out.'

'They were seeing each other behind my back for three months before Gemma came to me and confessed and...told me Andrew wanted to end it with me so they could get engaged straight away and start planning their future.'

'And you loved him.' Troy's gaze softened. 'That was a rough thing to go through.'

'I felt betrayed by Gemma, and by the rest of the family, because they got behind her and told me I had to just accept it and be happy for her when all I wanted was to be angry and hurt.' Oh, Stacie had felt so hurt, and hadn't she had that right?

'I didn't love Andrew as much as I thought I did, Troy.' She knew that now, too. 'I know now that I'll be able to be a good sister to Gemma again. It still stings to know that both my sisters could still take any man from me that they wanted.'

'Not any man.' The words rumbled from Troy's chest in a deep tone. 'I'm sorry you had those experiences, Stacie, and I wish your family had been a bit more understanding, but in the end Andrew Gale was a fool. He had the chance to have you at his side, and he tossed it away.'

Oh, Stacie loved Troy in that moment for making her feel so special, so appealing.

'It's time I stopped thinking about it and, rather than refusing to put myself out there again, have faith in myself and go after what I want—well, what I need in life.' It felt good to have got the words out.

It felt...freeing.

'You've come a long way.' Troy's words held praise.

'I admired that about you from when I first met you. That you'd picked up and moved and started a whole new life and you were making it work. You had your goals in place and enough determination and enthusiasm to see them through.'

A smile kicked up one side of his mouth. 'Right down to a designer pink tool-kit, a thirst for conquering DIY projects, and your gorgeous, ever-changing nails.'

'You've done the same, Troy.' Surely he could see that? 'You've started over. I didn't lose a career that I felt passionate about. Not in the way you did.'

He dipped his chin. 'Instead, you started to build one.'

That was true. Stacie nodded. 'Yes.'

'I said if Linda hadn't ended our relationship after my injury happened, I would have.' He seemed to force the words out. 'You've made me realise that way of thinking was flawed. My relationship with her was flawed, empty, and on the surface when it should have been rich and deep. I thought that was all I had to give. And Linda? I don't think she cared deeply for me, otherwise she'd have found it hard to step away in the way she did.'

'I don't want to play down your injury, Troy. I respect the loss it's brought to you, and that it impacts on your life every day.' Stacie just wished he could see his strength. 'But the first time I met you, I saw how determined you were, and how strong. And look at how you handled things today. You don't let anything stop you.'

'Sometimes it just slows me down a bit.' Troy nodded. 'You're right. I felt bitter about the injury because it meant loss of career and of the sense of family I had in the army, where I was among people that I felt understood me.'

'You said your parents travel a lot now that they're retired.'

'They're not a happy couple. Mum always tried to find emotional stability by trying to latch on to me for it. As a boy.'

'That made you shut down to protect yourself.'

'Yes. But I thought the feelings just weren't there. I believed Mum when she said that.' He drew a breath. 'I'm not knocking them, just telling you how that was.'

'I understand.' And Stacie did. 'We've both been through things that have shaped us, Troy.'

'I want to give all those unlocked parts of me to you, Stacie.' He uttered the words and his expression and the touch of his fingers against hers told her they were true to him.

That he cared. 'You're the most beautiful woman I've ever known, Stacie. Inside and out. To me, that's how you will always be.'

Stacie drew a tight breath. She should stop and think. She shouldn't commit herself to Troy if he couldn't care for her to the depth that she loved him. But he'd said those beautiful things, and it was plain he had meant them. And she wanted a chance to love him. Oh, she wanted that so much! 'If there's any chance—'

'If there's a chance that you might love—' He stopped.

Stacie's heart thundered. Had he just said what she thought he had said? 'I'm not sure if you mean…'

'I'm deep in love with you. That's what I mean.' He got to his feet, pulled her to her feet and his hands cupped her shoulders as he gazed into her face. 'I want to look at your face every day for the rest of my life. To become so familiar with each feature that I know each part of you better than I know myself. And when I've done that I want to start over and learn you all over again. I want to know you as well on the inside.'

'Troy?' Her heart slowed, and then rushed on a bursting beat.

His expression, his touch, the sincerity and hope and belief in his eyes, told it all. *He loved her.* Truly, as she loved him.

'I love you too, Troy.' The words burst from her. 'I knew it the morning after… I didn't know what to do.' She drew a breath. 'No; that isn't true. I was afraid to reach out for what I wanted with you. I thought you wouldn't want me, but then I wanted to fight for you if there was any chance.'

'You are a fighter, and I'm glad of that.' He cupped her face in his hands and closed his eyes and for a moment he simply breathed her in. 'Because I want you to fight to stay with me for always. To build a life with me. To sell dog-coats and grow almonds and survive floods, and look after muscle-dogs with beauty complexes and Houdini dogs wanting to escape all the time.'

It was Stacie's idea of heaven. 'Oh, Troy. I want that. I want it all.'

'And children.' His voice lowered an octave as he spoke the words. 'I want beautiful children with you. Daughters just like you.'

'And sons just like you.' Her voice choked on the words. 'Oh, Troy. I want sons just like you.'

She would have a niece or nephew first, and Stacie just smiled because it would be nice, but it was Troy's babies that she would carry the deepest in her heart.

Troy pressed his forehead to hers and inhaled. 'My mother might warn you to steer away from anything to do with me and tell you I'm cold.'

'She tried to fix her unhappiness by leaning on you emotionally.' Stacie said it gently, but it still had to be said. 'That was wrong of her, Troy.'

'Families aren't perfect, are they?' Troy lifted his forehead from hers and pressed his lips there instead. 'But I care about my parents, and they're not bad people. I think they're just not all that happy with each other.'

Stacie's hands crept around his middle. She was still struggling to believe this but, oh, she needed to, and touching him made it more possible to believe. '*We're* going to be happy, Troy. We're going to share emotionally and in every way. Support each other and go forward together.'

He tipped up her chin and looked deep into her eyes. 'Then marry me, Stacie Wakefield. Make me the happiest man in the world.'

'Oh, Troy.' She drew a shuddery breath. Their lips pressed together lightly, just once, and she spoke her answer against those lips she had dreamed from the start must be made for kisses. 'Yes. I will marry you and try to live up to your strength.'

Troy hushed her with a finger laying lightly against her lips. 'You don't need to try to match my strength. You already do.'

'And you don't ever need to worry about your injury with me.' Warmth crept into her face as she admitted, 'From the first day we met I saw the way you lived with those limitations and conquered them. I found you so attractive.'

Stacie's arms squeezed his waist as he pulled her tight against his hard body, and let her hair flow over the back of his hand where he cupped her neck.

'I want to make love with you.' He whispered the words against her neck.

'I want it too, Troy. I need you. You, and only you.'

Stacie took his hand. They left two dogs lying in front of a heater in Troy's living room, and she and Troy resumed their journey together.

* * * * *

CLASSIC

Quintessential, modern love stories
that are romance at its finest.

Harlequin® Romance

COMING NEXT MONTH
AVAILABLE MARCH 13, 2012

#4297 ONCE A COWBOY...
The Quilt Shop in Kerry Springs
Patricia Thayer

**#4297 PREGNANT WITH THE
PRINCE'S CHILD**
The Lost Princes of Ambria
Raye Morgan

**#4297 THE NANNY AND THE
BOSS'S TWINS**
The Nanny Handbook
Barbara McMahon

**#4297 INHERITED: EXPECTANT
CINDERELLA**
Myrna Mackenzie

#4297 BACK IN THE SOLDIER'S ARMS
Heroes Come Home
Soraya Lane

**#4297 THE INCONVENIENT LAWS
OF ATTRACTION**
Trish Wylie

You can find more information on upcoming Harlequin®
titles, free excerpts and more at www.Harlequin.com.

HRCNM0212

REQUEST YOUR FREE BOOKS!
2 FREE NOVELS PLUS 2 FREE GIFTS!

Harlequin Romance

From the Heart, For the Heart

YES! Please send me 2 FREE Harlequin® Romance novels and my 2 FREE gifts (gifts are worth about $10). After receiving them, if I don't wish to receive any more books, I can return the shipping statement marked "cancel". If I don't cancel, I will receive 6 brand-new novels every month and be billed just $4.09 per book in the U.S. or $4.49 per book in Canada. That's a savings of at least 14% off the cover price! It's quite a bargain! Shipping and handling is just 50¢ per book in the U.S. and 75¢ per book in Canada.* I understand that accepting the 2 free books and gifts places me under no obligation to buy anything. I can always return a shipment and cancel at any time. Even if I never buy another book, the two free books and gifts are mine to keep forever.

116/316 HDN FESE

Name _____ (PLEASE PRINT)

Address _____ Apt. #

City _____ State/Prov. _____ Zip/Postal Code

Signature (if under 18, a parent or guardian must sign)

Mail to the **Reader Service:**
IN U.S.A.: P.O. Box 1867, Buffalo, NY 14240-1867
IN CANADA: P.O. Box 609, Fort Erie, Ontario L2A 5X3

Not valid for current subscribers to Harlequin Romance books.

**Are you a subscriber to Harlequin Romance books
and want to receive the larger-print edition?**
Call 1-800-873-8635 or visit www.ReaderService.com.

* Terms and prices subject to change without notice. Prices do not include applicable taxes. Sales tax applicable in N.Y. Canadian residents will be charged applicable taxes. Offer not valid in Quebec. This offer is limited to one order per household. All orders subject to credit approval. Credit or debit balances in a customer's account(s) may be offset by any other outstanding balance owed by or to the customer. Please allow 4 to 6 weeks for delivery. Offer available while quantities last.

Your Privacy—The Reader Service is committed to protecting your privacy. Our Privacy Policy is available online at www.ReaderService.com or upon request from the Reader Service.

We make a portion of our mailing list available to reputable third parties that offer products we believe may interest you. If you prefer that we not exchange your name with third parties, or if you wish to clarify or modify your communication preferences, please visit us at www.ReaderService.com/consumerschoice or write to us at Reader Service Preference Service, P.O. Box 9062, Buffalo, NY 14269. Include your complete name and address.

HRI1B

Harlequin *Presents*

USA TODAY bestselling author

Carol Marinelli

begins a daring duet.

THE SECRETS
of
XANOS

Two brothers alike in charisma and power;
separated at birth and seeking revenge...

Nico has always felt like an outsider. He's turned his back on his
parents' fortune to become one of Xanos's most powerful exports
and nothing will stand in his way—until he stumbles
upon a virgin bride....

Zander took his chances on the streets rather than spending another
moment under his cruel father's roof. Now he is unrivaled in
business—and the bedroom! He wants the best people around him,
and Charlotte is the best PA! Can he tempt her
over to the dark side...?

A SHAMEFUL CONSEQUENCE
Available in March

AN INDECENT PROPOSITION
Available in April

HP13053

New York Times *and* USA TODAY *bestselling author*
Maya Banks presents book three in her miniseries
PREGNANCY˙& PASSION.

TEMPTED BY HER INNOCENT KISS

Available March 2012 from Harlequin Desire!

There came a time in a man's life when he knew he was well and truly caught. Devon Carter stared down at the diamond ring nestled in velvet and acknowledged that this was one such time. He snapped the lid closed and shoved the box into the breast pocket of his suit.

He had two choices. He could marry Ashley Copeland and fulfill his goal of merging his company with Copeland Hotels, thus creating the largest, most exclusive line of resorts in the world, or he could refuse and lose it all.

Put in that light, there wasn't much he could do except pop the question.

The doorman to his Manhattan high-rise apartment hurried to open the door as Devon strode toward the street. He took a deep breath before ducking into his car, and the driver pulled into traffic.

Tonight was the night. All of his careful wooing, the countless dinners, kisses that started brief and casual and became more breathless—all a lead-up to tonight. Tonight his seduction of Ashley Copeland would be complete, and then he'd ask her to marry him.

He shook his head as the absurdity of the situation hit him for the hundredth time. Personally, he thought William Copeland was crazy for forcing his daughter down Devon's throat.

Ashley was a sweet enough girl, but Devon had no desire

to marry anyone.

William had other plans. He'd told Devon that Ashley had no head for the family business. She was too softhearted, too naive. So he'd made Ashley part of the deal. The catch? Ashley wasn't to know of it. Which meant Devon was stuck playing stupid games.

Ashley was supposed to think this was a grand love match. She was a starry-eyed woman who preferred her animal-rescue foundation over board meetings, charts and financials for Copeland Hotels.

If she ever found out the truth, she wouldn't take it well.

And hell, he couldn't blame her.

But no matter the reason for his proposal, before the night was over, she'd have no doubts that she belonged to him.

What will happen when Devon marries Ashley?
Find out in Maya Banks's passionate new novel
TEMPTED BY HER INNOCENT KISS
Available March 2012 from Harlequin Desire!

Get swept away with author

CATHY GILLEN THACKER

and her new miniseries

Legends of Laramie County

On the Cartwright ranch, it's the women
who endure and run the ranch—and it's time for
lawyer Liz Cartwright to take over. Needing some help
around the ranch, Liz hires Travis Anderson, a fellow
attorney, and Liz's high-school boyfriend. Travis says
he wants to get back to his ranch roots, but Liz knows
Travis is running from something. Old feelings emerge
as they work together, but Liz can't help but wonder
if Travis is home to stay.

Reluctant Texas Rancher

Available March
wherever books are sold.